TREASURES OF CORNWALL

A Literary Anthology

T0347693

More regional anthologies
from Macmillan Collector's Library

Yorkshire: A Literary Landscape
edited by David Stuart Davies

TREASURES OF CORNWALL

A Literary Anthology

Edited and introduced by
LUKE THOMPSON

MACMILLAN COLLECTOR'S LIBRARY

This collection first published 2023 by Macmillan Collector's Library
an imprint of Pan Macmillan
The Smithson, 6 Briset Street, London EC1M 5NR
EU representative: Macmillan Publishers Ireland Ltd,
1st Floor, The Liffey Trust Centre, 117–126 Sheriff Street Upper,
Dublin 1, D01 YC43
Associated companies throughout the world
www.panmacmillan.com

ISBN 978-1-5290-9039-0

Selection, preface and author biographies © Luke Thompson 2023
Map artwork © Hemesh Alles

The permissions acknowledgements on p. 279 constitute an extension
of this copyright page.

1 3 5 7 9 8 6 4 2

A CIP catalogue record for this book is available from the British Library.

Typeset in Plantin by Jouve (UK), Milton Keynes
Printed and bound by TJ Books Ltd, Padstow, Cornwall PL28 8RW

Visit **www.panmacmillan.com** to read more
about all our books and to buy them.

Contents

CORNWALL

N

ATLANTIC OCEAN

Padstow

Perranporth

Trethosa

St Ives

Truro

Zennor

Camborne

Botallack

Carbis Bay

Penzance

Helston

St Michaels Mount

Falmouth

Poldhu

Lizard Peninsula

E

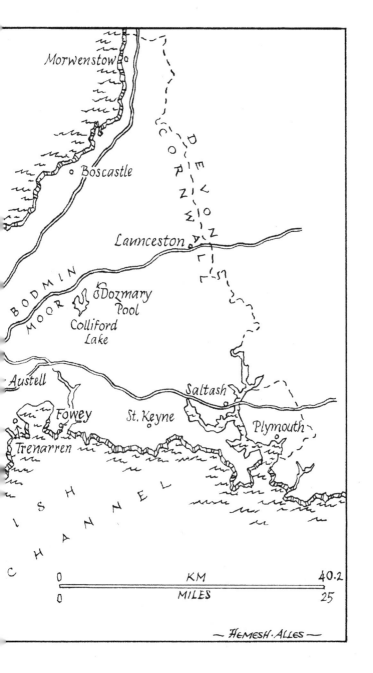

Morwenstow

Boscastle

CORNWALL

DEVON

Launceston

BODMIN MOOR

Dozmary Pool

Colliford Lake

Austell

Fowey

St. Keyne

Saltash

Plymouth

Trenarren

IRISH

CHANNEL

C

| 0 | KM | 40.2 |
| 0 | MILES | 25 |

— HEMESH·ALLES —

Preface

Welcome one and all to our tour of Cornwall. We'll be casting off in just a minute, so make yourselves as comfy as you can. I know, I know, the water's a bit bumpy but at least there's no rain. What, this? A little mizzle, that's all. You'll dry off soon enough.

Here we go. Heave away! Now what do you say to a song, you know, to pass the time?

> O rugged and bold are Cornwall's cliffs,
>   And rugged and bold are her men,
> Stalwart and true when there's work to do,
>   And heeding not where or when . . .

Look everyone, Cornwall ahead. We're nearly there. Land of moors and mines, Petrock and Piran, the knockers and the giants. Yes, that's right – *giants*. Wait until we get down west and you'll learn all about them. Giants, piskies, mermaids – you know them, I reckon. What of that wailing devil Tregeagle, or the fairies of Towednack? Well, it's a good job I'll be taking you to meet our storytellers!

These days we have as many storytellers as we once had saints and spriggans. Swarms of writerly folk scuttled in – William Golding up Truro way, Daphne du Maurier down in Fowey. We'll drop in on one or two of these recent settlers sure enough, but I want to show you a bit of old Cornwall too. The Cornwall of yesteryear – a place that both was and wasn't in a time when piskies and pilchards were plentiful and Cornwall was a mystery to English folk, a sort of wild place where they imagined all their fancies and fears might dwell, surrounded by the savage sea. In those days, folk might only know Cornwall to pass through on their way to the packet ships leaving Falmouth for Spain or Portugal, the Americas or the Caribbean.

The Cornwall I'll sing you is the Cornwall of the miner-poet John Harris and of the old vicar up Morwenstow who buried bodies wrecked on the beach; the Cornwall of King Arthur and Sir Tristan; the Cornwall of Jack the Giant Killer and of James Polkinghorne, our greatest wrestler since Corineus landed backalong. It's a Cornwall lived, a Cornwall imagined, and a Cornwall remembered in legend and song.

Speaking of song, I'd barely made a start on 'One and All' . . .

Braving the storm on ocean wave,
    Or toiling beneath the ground,
Wherever the spot, whatever his lot,
    The Cornishmen staunch is found . . .

Aha! Look! Our first narrator is back at the port. He'll follow us over. Not exactly a local, you'll notice, but he tells a good story. He's getting in with Mr Dawle, it looks like. Have you all met that Wilkie Collins?

TREASURES OF CORNWALL

A Literary Anthology

WILKIE COLLINS
(1824–1889)

Well, whether you have met Wilkie Collins or no, you're bound to have heard of some of his books; popular novels of sensation like *The Woman in White* and *The Moonstone*. But Wilkie Collins also wrote a lively traveller's account of Cornwall, his *Rambles Beyond Railways*, from a visit in 1850. This was before the railway line opened up Cornwall's tourist industry and before great bridges crossed the Tamar, which is why he's having to find himself a boat. Collins wanted, he says, to see 'the grand and varied scenery; the mighty Druid relics; the quaint legends; the deep, dark mines; the venerable remains of early Christianity; and the pleasant primitive population of Cornwall'. On the whole he enjoyed our 'primitive population', save for the people of Helston, whom he called a 'riotous and drunken set, the only bad specimens of people that I met with in Cornwall'.

The trip would inform his novels too, especially *Basil*, which reuses descriptions of Land's End's thatched cottages, gull's egg ornaments, the mist and mizzle.

The following extract finds Mr Collins kicking off from Plymouth on his way to Saltash, right at the beginning of his Cornwall adventure.

Oh, and the man alongside him? That's the artist Henry Brandling.

from Rambles Beyond Railways

We were lucky enough to commit ourselves, at once, to the guidance of the most amusing and original of boatmen. He was a fine, strong, swarthy fellow, with luxuriant black hair and whiskers, an irresistible broad grin, and a thoroughly good opinion of himself. He gave us his name, his autobiography, and his opinion of his own character, all in a breath. He was called William Dawle; he had begun life as a farm-labourer; then he had become a sailor in the Royal Navy, as a suitable change; now he was a licensed waterman, which was a more suitable change still; he was known all over the country; he would row against any man in England; he would take more care of us than he would of his own sons; and if we had five hundred guineas apiece in our knapsacks, he could keep no stricter watch over them than he was determined to keep now. Such was this phœnix of boatmen—under such unexceptionable auspices did we start for the shores of Cornwall.

The calm summer evening drew near its close, as we began to move through the water. The broad orb of the moon was rising dim behind us, above the dark majestic trees of Mount Edgecombe. Already, the houses of Devonport looked pale and indistinct as we left them behind us. The innumerable masts, the lofty men-of-war hulks, the drooping sails of smaller vessels—all the thickly grouped objects of the great port through which we were proceeding—assumed a solemn stillness and repose under the faint light that was now shining over them. On this wide scene, at other hours so instinct in all its parts with bustle and animation, nothing spoke now of life and action—save the lights which occasionally broke forth from houses on the hill at our side, or the small boats passing at intervals over the smooth water, and soon mysteriously lost to view behind the hull of a man-of-war, or in the deep shadows of the river's distant banks.

In front of us, the last glories of day still lingered in the west. Here, the sky was yet bright and warm to look on, though the sun had gone down, and, even now, the evening star was plainly visible. In this part of the landscape, the wooded hills rose dark and grand against their transparent background of light. Where the topmost trees grew thinnest, long strips of rosy sky appeared through their interstices; the water beyond us was tinged in one place with all the colours of the prism, in another with the palest and coldest blue—even the wet mud-banks, left by the retiring tide, still glittered with silvery brightness in the waning light. While, adding solemnity and mystery to all beside, the great hulks, painted pale yellow and anchored close in against the black trees, lay before us still and solitary, touched alike by the earliest moonbeams of night and the last sunlight of day. As the twilight gloom drew on—as the impressive tranquillity of the whole scene deepened and deepened gradually, until not even the distant barking of a dog was now heard from the land, or the shrill cry of a sea-bird from the sky—the pale massy hulls of the old war-ships around and beyond us, assumed gradually a spectral and mysterious appearance, until they looked more like water-monsters in repose than the structures of mortal hands, and the black heights behind them seemed like lairs from which they had issued under cover of the night!

It was such an evening, and such a view, as I shall never forget. After enjoying the poetry and beauty of the scene uninterruptedly, for some time, we were at length recalled to practical matters of business by a species of adjuration suddenly addressed to us by that prince of British boatmen, Mr. William Dawle. Resting impressively upon his oars, and assuming a deplorable expression of countenance, he begged to be informed, whether we really wished him to "row his soul out any longer against tide?"—we might laugh, but would we be so kind as to step forward a minute and feel his shirt sleeves?—If we were resolved to go on, he was ready; for had he not told us that he would row against any man in England?—but he felt it due to his position as a licensed waterman, having the eyes of the public on him, and courting inspection, to inform us that "in three parts of an hour, and no mistake," the tide would run up; and that there was a place not far off, called Saltash—a most beautiful and interesting place, where we could get good beer. If we waited there for the turn of the tide, no racehorse that ever was foaled would take us to St. Germans so fast as he would row us. In short, the point was, would we mercifully "spare his shoulders," or not?

As we belonged to the sauntering and vagabond order of travellers, and cared very little in how roundabout a manner we reached our destination, we inclined to the side of mercy, and spared the shoulders of Mr. William Dawle; who, thereupon, reckless of the state of his shirt-sleeves, began to row again with renewed and alarming energy. Now, he bent forward over the oars, as if he was about to fall upon us—and now, he lay back from them, horizontal, and almost lost to view in the dim light. We passed, triumphantly, every boat proceeding in our direction; we brushed, at hairbreadth distances, by vessels at anchor and stakes planted in shallow water. Suddenly, what seemed to be a collection of mud hovels built upon mud, appeared in sight; shortly afterwards, our boat was grounded among a perfect legion of other boats; and the indefatigable Dawle, jumping up nimbly, seized our knapsacks and handed us out politely into the mud. We had arrived at that "beautiful and interesting place," Saltash.

There was no mistaking the tavern. The only light on shore gleamed from the tavern window; and, judging by the criterion of noise, the whole local population seemed to be collected within the tavern walls. We opened the door; and found ourselves in a small room, filled with shrimpers, sailors, fishermen and watermen, all "looming large" through a fog of tobacco, and all chirping merrily over their cups; while the hostess sat apart on a raised seat in a corner, calm and superior amidst the hubbub, as Neptune himself, when he rose to the surface to save the pious Eneas from shipwreck, at the crisis of the storm. As there was no room for us in this festive hall, we were indulged in the luxury of a private apartment, where Mr. Dawle proceeded to "do the honours" of Saltash, by admonishing the servant to be particular about the quality of the ale she brought, dusting chairs with the crown of his hat, proposing toasts, snuffing the candle briskly with his fingers, and performing other pleasant social attentions of a similar nature. Having, as he imagined, sufficiently propitiated us by this course of conduct, he started an entirely new proposition—which bore reference, however, to the old subject of mercifully sparing his shoulders, and was expressed to the following effect:—Might he go now, and fetch his "missus," who lived hard by? She was the very nicest and strongest woman in Saltash; was able to row almost as well as *he* could, and would help him materially in getting to St. Germans; but perhaps we objected to admit her into the boat? We had but to say the word, if we did; and from that moment forth, he was dumb on the subject for ever.

How could we resist this most irresistible of boat-men? There was something about his inveterate good-humour and inveterate idleness, his comical variations backwards and forwards between great familiarity and great respect, his honesty on one point (he asked us no more than his proper fare in the first instance) and his manœuvring on another, that would have cajoled a Cynic into complacency. Besides, our innate sentiments of gallantry forbade the thought of objecting to the company and assistance of Mrs. William Dawle! So, we sent

6

the fortunate spouse of this strong and useful woman, to seek her forthwith—and forthwith did he return, with a very remarkable species of "missus," in the shape of a gigantic individual of the male sex—the stoutest, strongest, and hairiest man I ever saw—who entered, exhaling a relishing odour of shrimps, with his shirt-sleeves rolled up to his shoulders! "Gentlemen both, good evening," said this urbane giant, looking dreamily forward two feet over our heads, and then settling himself solemnly on a bench—never more to open his lips in our presence!

Our worthy boatman's explanation of the phenomenon he had thus presented to us, involved some humiliating circumstances. His "missus" had flatly refused to aid her lord and master in the exertion of rowing, and had practically carried out her refusal by immediately going to bed before his face. As for the shrimp-scented giant, Mr. Dawle informed me (in a whisper) that his name was "Dick;" that he had met him outside, and had asked him to favour us with his company, because he was a very amusing man, if we could only bring him out; and was capable of beguiling the time, while we were waiting for the tide, by an excellent story or two. Presuming that a fresh supply of ale was all that was wanting to develop the latent humour of our new friend, we ordered a second quart; but it unhappily produced no effect. (It would have required, I am inclined to think, a gallon to have attained the desired result.) "Dick" sat voiceless and vacant, staring steadily at the candle, and occasionally groaning softly to himself, as if he had something dreadful on his mind and dared not disburthen it in company. Abandoning, therefore, in despair, all hope of enjoying the comic amusement which had been promised us, we left our bulky humorist still silent and portentous as a Quaker at "meeting"—proof alike against the potency of the ale and the blandishments of Mr. Dawle—and went out at the last moment to make our observations on Saltash by night.

The moonlight gave us very little assistance, as we groped our way up a steep hill, down which two rows of old cottages seemed to be gradually toppling into the water beyond. Here and there, an open door showed us a Rembrandt scene—a glowing red fire brilliantly illuminating the face of a woman cooking at it, or the forms of ragged children asleep on the hearth; and leaving all beside—figures, furniture, and rough raftered ceiling—steeped in grand and gloomy shadow. There were plenty of loose stones in the road, to trip up the feet of inquisitive strangers; there was plenty of stinking water bubbling musically down the kennel; and there were no lamps of any kind, to throw the smallest light upon any topographical subject of inquiry whatever. When I have proceeded thus far, and have further informed the curious in such matters, that Charles the Second conferred upon Saltash the inestimable blessing of a Mayor and six Aldermen—that it had the honour and advantage, before the Reform Bill, of sending two members to Parliament—and that it still possesses various municipal privileges of an equally despotic and lucrative nature, connected with oyster-fisheries, anchorage, salvage, ferries, and market-tolls—I have said all that I can about Saltash; and must request the reader's permission to return to the tavern without further delay.

Here, the scene had changed since our departure. The jovial company of the public room had penetrated into the private parlour. In the midst of the crowd stood Mr. Dawle, haranguing, with the last glass of ale in his hand; by his side was his son, who had been bribed, for the paltry consideration of sixpence, to relieve his parent's shoulders by helping to row us to St. Germans; and, on the old bench, in the old position, with the old fixed stare straight into the flame of the candle, sat the imperturbable "Dick"—stolid and gloomy as ever, in the midst of the festive uproar. It was now high time to proceed. So we gave the word to depart. But an unexpected obstacle impeded us at the doorway. All the women who could squeeze themselves into the passage, suddenly fell down at our feet, and began scrubbing the dust off our shoes with the corners of their aprons; informing us, at the same time, in shrill chorus, that this was an ancient custom to which we must submit; and that any stranger who entered a Saltash house, and had his shoes dusted by Saltash women, was expected to pay his footing, by giving a trifle—say sixpence—for liquor; after which, he became a free and privileged citizen for life. As I do not remember that this interesting custom is mentioned among the other municipal privileges of Saltash, in any Itineraries or Histories of Cornwall, I communicate it, in all humility, to any antiquarian gentleman who may be disposed to make a scientific use of it, for the benefit of the community at large.

On departing at last for St. Germans, grave doubts arose in our minds, as to the effect which Dawle's potations of ale might have on his professional exertions as a licensed waterman. We were immediately relieved, however, by finding that what he had drunk had influenced him for good, rather than for evil—he talked less, and rowed more. Smoothly and swiftly we glided through the still water. The tide had now been flowing for some time; the arm of the sea, up which we were proceeding, was in many places more than half a mile across; on the broad, smooth surface of the stream, the moonlight lay fair and unruffled; the woods clothing the hills on each side, grew down to the water's edge, and were darkly reflected, all along, in solemn, winding shapes. Sometimes we passed an old ship, rotten and mastless, anchored solitary, midway between land and land. Sometimes we saw, afar off, a light in a fisherman's cottage among the trees; but we met no boats, saw no living beings, heard no voices, on our lonely way. It was nearly midnight before we reached the landing-place; got out in the mud again here; and, guided by our trusty boatman, began to ascend the hill-path that led to St. Germans.

ROBERT SOUTHEY
(1774–1843)

Let's pick up the trail and head down to St Keyne for a spot of poetry. It would be easy to miss this little well, tucked away along back roads between Looe and Liskeard, but it captured the Poet Laureate Robert Southey's attention.

In actual fact, Southey hadn't visited the well when he wrote this poem, and he wouldn't visit Cornwall until much later, when he made an attempt on some of the sights during a very wet winter, but he had read the account of Cornish poet-historian Richard Carew in his 1602 *Survey of Cornwall*. According to Carew, the well of St Keyne has the power to make a newlywed the master or mistress of their spouse:

> The quality, that man or wife,
> Whose chance, or choice attaines,
> First of this sacred streame to drinke,
> Thereby the mastry gaines.

Many of the wells of Cornwall have healing or magical properties, but taking charge of your other half has to be unique to St Keyne.

The Well of St Keyne

A well there is in the west country,
 And a clearer one never was seen;
There is not a wife in the west country
 But has heard of the Well of St. Keyne.

An oak and an elm-tree stand beside,
 And behind doth an ash-tree grow,
And a willow from the bank above
 Droops to the water below.

A traveller came to the Well of St. Keyne;
 Joyfully he drew nigh,
For from cock-crow he had been travelling,
 And there was not a cloud in the sky.

He drank of the water so cool and clear,
 For thirsty and hot was he;
And he sat down upon the bank
 Under the willow-tree.

There came a man from the house hard by,
 At the Well to fill his pail;
On the Well-side he rested it,
 And he bade the Stranger hail.

"Now art thou a bachelor, Stranger? quoth he;
    "For an if thou hast a wife,
The happiest draught thou hast drank this day
    That ever thou didst in thy life.

"Or has thy good woman, if one thou hast,
    Ever here in Cornwall been?
For an if she have, I'll venture my life,
    She has drank of the Well of St. Keyne."

"I have left a good woman who never was here,"
    The Stranger he made reply;
"But that my draught should be the better for that,
    I pray you answer me why."

"St. Keyne," quoth the Cornish-man, "many a time
    Drank of this crystal Well;
And before the Angel summon'd her,
    She laid on the water a spell.

"If the Husband of this gifted Well
    Shall drink before his Wife,
A happy man thenceforth is he,
    For he shall be Master for life.

"But if the Wife should drink of it first,—
    God help the Husband then!"
The Stranger stoop'd to the Well of St. Keyne,
    And drank of the water again.

"You drank of the Well, I warrant, betimes?"
　　He to the Cornish-man said:
But the Cornish-man smiled as the Stranger spake,
　　And sheepishly shook his head.

"I hasten'd as soon as the wedding was done,
　　And left my Wife in the porch;
But i' faith she had been wiser than me,
　　For she took a bottle to church."

JOHN PENWARNE
(1758–1838)

If you know only two legends of Cornwall, one of them will be that of Tregeagle. Like all the best tales, Tregeagle is told in different ways. This version was written by John Penwarne and published in his little 1807 *Contemplation*. It's one of the more elaborate and fantastical versions, with Tregeagle an ambitious shepherd rather than a corrupt land manager, but it maintains Tregeagle's pact with the devil and the price he has to pay.

To this day, in the wildest of tempests you can still hear Tregeagle screaming as he's chased across Cornwall by the Devil and his dogs.

Tregeagle, *from* Contemplation

I

In Cornwaile's fam'd land, bye the poole on the moore,
    Tregeagle the wickede did dwelle;
He once was a shepherde contented and poore;
But growing ambytious and wishing for more,
    Sad fortune the shepherde befelle.

2

One nyghte, all alone, as he cross'd the wylde heathe
    To drive his scant flocke to the folde,
All nature was stille, the wynds scarcely breathe
O'er the moone silver'd hilles and the vallies beneath,
    As he cast his eye over the wolde.

3

"Ah! why shoulde I live bye hard laboure"—quothe he,
    "And be helde bye the riche in dysdayne!
"I wish"—quothe Tregeagle—"for all that I see,
"Oh then what a happye great man I shoulde be!
    "When lorde of extensive domaine."

4

Nowe scarce had he utter'd hys impious breath,
　　When the wolves they howl'd wildlye and loude;
The wyndes sadly syghing swept over the heath,
As nature awoke frome the styllness of deathe;
　　And the moone hyd her head in a cloude.

5

When suddaine he saw, midst the gloome of the nyghte,
　　A figure gygantick advance;
His hayre bristled up as he view'd the felle Spryte,
Who seemed in form to be armed as a knyghte,
　　And he wielded an ebonye lance.

6

All blacke was the gaunte steede on whych he dyd ryde;
　　A sable plume shadow'd his heade;
And blacke was his armoure, wyth bloode all bedy'de;
And blacke was the bugle that hung bye hys syde,
　　Which no mortale mighte hear without dreade.

7

Two dogges fierce and felle, and whych never knew
　　　feare,
　　Did run hys fleete courser before;

Their forms were all hydeous, and grislye their haire,
And thro' their lanke sydes their sharpe ribs did
    appeare,
  And their mouthes were stille dripping with gore.

8

Then thus spake Tregeagle—"who arte thou Syr
    Knyghte?
  "And where at this tyme dost thou wende?
"Ah, why dost thou wander alone thro' the nyghte?
"And why dost thou harrowe my soule wyth affryghte?
  "Or what does thy coming portende?"

9

The Knyghte nothing spake, but he leap'd wyth a bound
  From offe hys hyghe steede (with a frowne)
And as he alitte on the tremblinge grounde,
His armoure clank'd hollowe, a terrible sounde,
  And at length, thus he spake to the Clowne.

10

"Say what dydst thou wysh for thou tremblinge knave?
  "But thy wyshes are known unto mee;
"I give my consent then, if thou arte my slave;
"Longe life to enjoye too, thy wysh thou shalt have,
  "And an hundrede years give I to thee.

"I'll builde thee a castle, soe fair and soe fyne,
  "Arounde it green forrests I'll reare,
"And vassals and serving men too shall bee thyne;
"And thy halle all wyth golde and wyth sylver shall
      shyne,
  "And wyth *Syr* shall bee greeted thyne eare.

"And when thy longe terme shall be passed awaye,
  "At thy lot wilt thou never repine?
"And wilt thou be ready the boone to repaye?
"Speake boldlye, Tregeagle! pray what doste thou saye?
  "Shalle thy soule and thy bodye be mine?"

"A bargaine! a bargaine!" then said he aloude,
  "At my lot I wille never repyne:
"I sweare to observe it, I sweare bye the roode,
"And am readye to seale and to sygne withe my bloode:
  "Both my soule and my bodye are thyne."

The Spryte grinn'd soe horrid, and said—"that wille
      bynde
  "Bothe thy soule and thy bodye my righte:"

Then mounting his courser as fleete as the wynde;
And whilst his grymme hell houndes ran yelpinge
    behinde,
  He was loste in the gloome of the nyghte.

15

Oh, then hys dreade bugle he wynded soe shrille,
  Soe as all mortale ears to astounde;
The vallies all trembled, and shooke was eache hylle,
The wolves ceas'd to howle, and wyth terrour lay stylle,
  Whyle Tregeagle felle flat on the grounde.

16

There in a deade sleepe all intranced he laye,
  Spelle bounde bye the arte of the Spryghte;
Nor awake untill morne in her mantel of graye,
With ruddy handes open'd the portalles of day,
  And dispell'd the darke mysts of the nyghte.

17

Then upsprange Tregeagle no longer a clowne,
  But cloathed in gorgeous attyre;
And proud wavinge forrests the hylls all dyd crowne,
Whych erst was a bare and a barren bleake downe,
  And much dyd Tregeagle admire.

Where Dozmarê Lake its darke waters did roll,
    A castle nowe reared its heade,
Wythe manye a turrete soe statelye and talle,
And manye a warden dyd walke on its walle,
    All splendidly cloathed in rede.

And manye a vassale dyd hayle hym "Syr Knighte,"
    And doffinge theire caps bowed lowe;
And muche Syr Tregeagle was pleas'd wythe the syghte,
While inwardlye swellinge wyth pryde and delyghte,
    He into hys castle dyd goe.

Then proudlye advauncinge he enter'd the halle
    With golde and with sylver bedyghte;
Frome the loftye roofe manye gaye banners dyd falle,
And bryghte suites of armoure did hange on eache walle,
    Was ever so gorgeous a syghte!

And there the gaye servinge men bowinge profounde,
    Obsequious dyd waite hys commande;
And manye faire damsels dyd stande hym arounde,

Who modestlye bent theire bryghte eyes to the
        grounde;
    Ah, who coulde such beautye wythstande!

22

The Mynstrel sweete musyck drewe forth from hys lyre,
    Whych ravysh'd the soule with delyghte;
The Knyghte treads on aire and his soule is on fyre,
And much he the skylle of the Harper admyres,
    For he sunge forthe the prayse of the Knyghte.

23

And manye a steed in hys stables were seene,
    All fitted for chace or for warre;
Withe manye bolde Huntesmen all cloathed in greene,
At their sydes hunge theire bugles of sylver soe sheene,
    Whych runge thro' the forrests a-farre.

24

Nowe oft woulde the Knyghte, on his courser soe faire,
    Followe swifte the fleete houndes and the horne,
To rouse the grymme wolfe frome hys secrete laire,
Or pursue the lyghte bounds of the tremblynge deere,
    As he brush'd the bryghte dewes of the morne.

But tyme flew awaye wyth the wyndes winged speede,
    Tregeagle ne'er notyc'd its flyghte;
But he marked each daye wyth some damnable deede,
Some mansyon muste burne or some traveller bleede,
    Or hatefulle that daye toe hys syghte.

26

It chaunced one evenynge as homewarde he wendes,
    Deepe mutter'd the hagg of the storme,
Earthe trembles, as boundynge the skyes she ascendes,
The welkyn acrosse her blacke wynges she extendes,
    And nature wyth darkness deformes.

27

And nowe the bolde Hunters they stoode all aghaste,
    Theire stoute heartes wyth feare overaw'd;
The rede lyghtnings glared, the rayne pour'd faste,
And loude howl'd the Demons that rode on the blaste,
    And Terrour the tempeste bestrode!

28

When swyfte frome the woode, and all wylde wyth
    affryghte,
    A Damsele advauncyng they spyed;

All whyte were her garments, her palfrye was whyte,
Wyth sylver and golde, and wyth jeweles bedyghte,
   And a little Page rode bye her syde.

29

"Oh, save me! Oh, save me! Syr Knyghte"—then she
     say'd,
   "Oh, let me thy succoure obtaine!
"Ah, where from the storme shall I shelter my heade?
"My spirits are synkyng with horrour and dreade,
   "And my garments are drenched wyth rayne.

30

"My poor little Page too, wyth terroure dothe quake,
   "Tho' ne'er little Page was more bolde:"—
"Ah, Mistress deare, I woulde dye for youre sake!
"It is not wyth feare that I shiver and shake,
   "But I shake wyth the wet and the colde."

31

"See yon'," sayd the Knyghte, "where mye castle
     dothe reare,
   "Thyther hasten faire ladye wyth me,
"And there we all soone will thy little Page cheere;
"Brighte damsels I've manye all modeste and faire,
   "Sweete Ladye to waite upon thee."

Nowe quickly they rode—and the drawe bridge let
    downe,
  They into the castle repayre;
And cheerfulle the fyres nowe blaz'd in the halle;
Tregeagle aloude for hys Damsels dyd calle,
  Hys Damsels soe lovelye and faire.

Some wayte on the Lady, some kyndlye are led
  To make the younge Urchyn their care;
Where lovelye he sat wyth his cheeks rosye rede;
And lyke a wet rosebude, he hunge downe hys heade,
  Whyle they wrunge forthe the rayne from hys haire.

"Nowe saye little Page," said a Damsel soe mylde,
  "And quicklye unto us declare,
"Why thro' the darke forreste soe savage and wylde,
"Thou rangedst at nyghte, who art yet but a chylde?
  "And who is thy Lady soe faire?"

"Her father's Earl Cornwaile—I weene that hys name,
  "Can never sounde straunge to youre eare;
"For large hys possessyons and wyde is hys fame,

"And I am her Page, and Roberto's mye name,
  "And they call her Goonhylda the fair."

36

"Thys mornynge, frome Dunevyd Castle soe stronge,
  "We came forthe, e'er the sunn shew'd hys face;
"For she loves wyth her trayne the greene forrests
      amonge,
"To rouse the fleete deere, and the vallies alonge
  "To pursue, the keene joyes of the chase.

37

"To daye, we left all oure companyons behynde,
  "And involv'd in the mysts of the hylle;
"To trace backe oure steps we in vaine were inclyn'd,
"When the shoutes of the Hunters we hearde in the
      wynde,
  "And the bugle blewe cleerlye and shrylle.

38

"Then we hytherwarde sped, all deceyv'd bye the sounde,
  "In hopes oure companyons to fynde;
"When the howlinge storme shooke the vast forreste
      arounde,
"From the rayne we soughte shelter but none coulde
      be founde,
  "Till we met wyth youre master soe kynde."

Then Goonhylda came forth—lyke a beautiful flower,
 And all in fresh garments array'd;
She seem'd a tall lyllye, refresh'd by a shower,
Tregeagle he gazed, for ne'er 'till that houre
 Had he seene such a beautiful Mayde.

40

"Thankes gentle Syr Knyghte," sayd Goonhylda
  the fair,
 "While modestye mantl'd her cheeke,
"Your guests for the nyghte we must be, Syr, I fear,
"Whylst mye father a preye to sad griefe and despayre,
 "In vaine hys Goonhylda wyll seek."

41

"I am proud of my gueste," Syr Tregeagle reply'd,
 "And praye fairest Ladye don't grieve;
"A messengere quicke to youre fathere shall ryde.
"To tell hym noe ill does hys daughter betyde,
 "And hys breast frome its terroure relieve."

42

Whyle thus wyth faire speeches soe courteous and
  kynde,
 Hymselfe to the Mayde he address'd;

To gloome, and to thoughtfulness seem'd much
    inclyn'd
And, if that the countenance speaketh the mynde,
  Darke deedes he revolv'd in hys breaste.

PART THE SECOND

I

Whyle sweete slept Goonhylda, of beautye the pryde,
  The Earle was absorbed in griefe;
For no messengere fleete to hys castle dyd ryde,
To saye, that no ill dyd hys darlynge betyde,
  And to gyue hys fond bosome reliefe.

2

All nyghte hys lone chambere, he pac'd to and fro;
  As he lysten'd, no sounde coulde he heare,
But the blaste whych against hys darke wyndowes dyd
    blowe,
Hys aged breaste heaved wyth sorrowe and woe,
  Till he saw the greye mornyng appear.

3

Wyth hys knyghtes, and esquyres, and servying men all,
  Then forthe frome hys castle dyd ryde;

Midst the forreste soe wylde on Goonhylda did call,
But dyre forebodings hys hearte dyd appalle,
    When noughte but the echoes reply'd.

4

At length to the plaine he emerg'd from the woode;
    For a father, alas, what a syghte!
There laye her fayre garments all drenched in bloode:
Her palfrye all torne in the darke crymsone floode,
    Bye the rav'nous beasts of the nyghte.

5

Soft eyed Pytye descende o'er the heart rending syghte,
    Be wydely extended thy veyle;
For I weene it is past learned Clerke to indyghte,
Or the pen or the pencile, to paynte or to wryte,
    What a fond tender father muste feele.

6

And nowe let's returne to that Traytour soe vyle,
    Darke projects revolv'd in hys breaste,
Whylst hys hearte was envelop'd in fraude and in guyle,
He borrowed kynde Hospytalitie's smyle,
    And thus he Goonhylda address'd:—

7

"Fair Mayden, than floweres the fairest most fayre;
  "Of demeanoure soe modeste and sweete;
"O say! may a Knyghte of possessyons so rare!
"Presume, that both them and hymselfe, to declare,
  "Deare Layde, are caste at youre feete."

8

Wythe a blushe on her cheeke, then Goonhylda reply'd,
  "I ill shoulde youre kindness requyte,
"Shoulde I treate you, Syr Knyghte, or wyth scorn or
      wyth pryde,
"Or the state of my hearte shoulde I stryve, Sir, to hyde,
  "I'm alreadye betroth'd to a knyghte.

9

"Now faire is the daye, and refulgente the morne;
  "And fayne woulde I haste to departe;
"That no longer my fonde partiale father may mourne,
"And no longer in vayne wayte Goonhylda's retourne,
  "Whose absence muste wrynge hys kynde hearte."

10

The Knyghte smylde insidious—and bente hys darke
      browe:
  "Faire Ladye you cannot goe hence:

"There are robbers abroade in the forreste I trowe;
"Besides, my sweete Damsele I boldlye avowe,
    "Wyth youre presence I cannot dyspence."

11

"Then am I a pris'ner?"—Goonhylda reply'd—
    (Indignante beholdynge the Knyghte)
"But soone shall the strength of thy castle be try'd
"And thynkest thou longe frome Earle Cornwaile
        to hyde,
    "A daughtere hys pryde and delyghte."

12

"Ah, vaine expectatione, fayre Ladye!" he sayd,
    "Thy father hopes not thy retourne;
"Alreadye he thynkes, that thy bloode has been shed
"Bye the beastes of the forreste; and thynkyng thee
        deade,
    "He is gone to hys castle to mourne."

13

Nowe little Roberto, tho' fewe were hys yeares,
    Yet cunning and shrewde was the boye;
Where he sat in a corner, thys speech overheares,
And faythfulle as swyfte to the stable repayres,
    And seyzes hys courser wyth joye.

14

From the castle he steals, and the forreste he gaynes,
   Resolv'd to averte her sad fate:
Nowe spurring, and gyvyng his fleete horse the reines,
Ere the soft tears of evenyng had spangled the plaines,
   Blewe hys horne at Duneved's high gate.

15

"Oh, hasten Earle Cornwaile! oh, hasten!" he cryd,
   "Thy peerless Goonhylda's in thralle;
"Bye a recreante Knyghte is thy powere defy'd!
"Bye force Syr Tregeagle woulde make her hys bryde!
   "And he keepes her wythin hys stronge walle!"

16

"For thy newes little Robert, oh, faire thee befalle,
   "Tho' bitter and sweete, little Page,
"Mye Goonhylda then lives! tho' a traytoure inthralls,
"But soone wyll I thundere arounde hys stronge walles,
   "The caytiffe I burne to engage!"

17

Then he drewe forth hys horsemen soe valyaunte
      and bolde;
   "And gyve me my armoure," he said,
"My frame can sustayne it, tho' wythered and olde,

"And my hande in its graspe, stylle the faulchyon can
     holde,
   "When a Daughtere's cause calls for its ayde.

18

"To horse little Robert! to horse againe flye!
   "Tho' tyred thou sorelye muste be;
"But I knowe for thy Mystress thou'dst readylye dye,
"And for thy rewarde I will make thee bye 'nd bye,
   "A Squyre of highest degree."

19

Nowe thro' the darke nyghte, over forreste and moore,
   They bye theyre fleete coursers are borne;
While little Roberto rode blythsome before,
And ere the greye morn peep'd the easterne hills o'er,
   At Tregeagle's gate sounded hys horne.

20

All is silente wythin, and the styllness of deathe
   The darke frowning toweres surroundes;
When they heard, and eache—listenyng suspended
     his breath,
They heard the shrylle blaste from the farre dystaunte
     heath!
   Whych the eares of all mortals confounds!

They hearde the Blacke Hunter! and dreade shooke
    each mynde,
  Heartes sanke that had never knowne feare:
They hearde the Blacke Hunter's dreade voyce in the
    wynde!
They hearde hys curste hell-houndes runn yelpyng
    behynde,
  And his steede thundered loude on the eare!

22

And nowe he appear'd thro' the gloome, of the nyghte;
  Hys plume, seem'd a cloude in the skyes;
His forme the darke mists of the hylles to the syghte;
And as from a furnace shootes forth the rede lyghte,
  Soe glared the fierce beams of hys eyes!

23

He blewe from hys bugle soe dreadeful a blaste,
  Hys dogges howlyng hydeous the whyle,
That all Nature trembled and shooke as aghaste!
And from the hygh walles the huge battlementes braste!
  Fell downe from the totteryng pyle.

"Come forth Syr Tregeagle!"—in thundere, he cried,
    "Come forth, and submit to thy fate!
"Thy tyme is expyred!—to me thou arte tyde!
"Wythyn thy dark castle in vayne thou wouldst hyde:
    "Come forth! for here endeth thy date!"

25

Then forth came Tregeagle all palsyed with fear,
    And fayne woulde more favoure have founde;
But loude roar'd the thundere, and swyfte thro' the ayre
The rede bolte of vengeaunce shot forth wyth a glare,
    And strooke hym a corpse to the grounde!

26

Then from the blake corpse a pale Spectre appear'd,
    And hyed him awaye thro' the nyghte,
When quickely the yelpes of the hell houndes are
        hearde,
And to the pursuite bye the bugle are cheer'd,
    Whyle behynde thunderes after the Spryte.

27

And nowe ruddy mornyng agayne gylds the skyes;
    The hellysh inchauntmente is o'er:
The forreste and castle no more meete theyre eyes;

35

But where from greene woodes, its bryghte turretes
    dyd rise,
  Nowe spreades the darke poole on the moore.

28

And neare its dreare margyn a Mayden was seene,
    Unhurted! Goonhylda the fayre;
For stylle Guardyan Angels dyd keepe her I weene,
And neare her gay palfrye in trappyngs soe sheene,
    Whych late torne by wolves dyd appeare.

29

Earle Cornwaile rejoycyng, now thanked that powere
    That dyd hys Goonhylda restore;
And ofte hys olde Mynstrelle, at Eve's sober houre,
Beneath the darke walles of Dunevyd's greye towere,
    Sunge the Tale of the poole on the moore.

30

And stylle, as the Trav'lere pursues hys lone waye
    In horroure, at nyghte o'er the waste,
He heares Syr Tregeagle wyth shriekes rushe awaye,
He heares the Blacke Hunter pursuing hys preye,
    And shrynkes at hys bugle's dreade blaste.

DAPHNE DU MAURIER
(1907–1989)

Let us head back to the coast. Fowey will be nice about now and we can hear from Daphne du Maurier. She lived all along this bit of Cornwall, first over the river there at Bodinnick, then around the headland at Menabilly and Kilmarth House. Grand places.

You might have heard of this story: 'The Birds'. Alfred Hitchcock based a film on it, only instead of the film being set in Cornwall, like the story, he set it in California. And instead of farm labourers it was high society. At least he kept those grumpy birds though.

I'd say du Maurier's short stories have some of her most inventive writing. One moment a patient is recovering from surgery and finds the people around her all have animal heads; the next a man's wife haunts her widow as a vengeful tree. They're great fun.

from 'The Birds'

On December the third the wind changed overnight and it was winter. Until then the autumn had been mellow, soft. The leaves had lingered on the trees, golden red, and the hedgerows were still green. The earth was rich where the plough had turned it.

Nat Hocken, because of a war-time disability, had a pension and did not work full-time at the farm. He worked three days a week, and they gave him the lighter jobs: hedging, thatching, repairs to the farm buildings.

Although he was married, with children, his was a solitary disposition; he liked best to work alone. It pleased him when he was given a bank to build up, or a gate to mend at the far end of the peninsula, where the sea surrounded the farm land on either side. Then, at midday, he would pause and eat the pasty that his wife had baked for him, and sitting on the cliff's edge would watch the birds. Autumn was best for this, better than spring. In spring the birds flew inland, purposeful, intent; they knew where they were bound, the rhythm and ritual of their life brooked no delay. In autumn those that had not migrated overseas but remained to pass the winter were caught up in the same driving urge, but because migration was denied them followed a pattern of their own. Great flocks of them came to the peninsula, restless, uneasy, spending themselves in motion; now wheeling, circling in the sky, now settling to feed on the rich new-turned soil, but even when they fed it was as though they did so without hunger, without desire. Restlessness drove them to the skies again.

Black and white, jackdaw and gull, mingled in strange partnership, seeking some sort of liberation, never satisfied, never still. Flocks of starlings, rustling like silk, flew to fresh pasture, driven by the same necessity of movement, and the smaller birds, the finches and the larks, scattered from tree to hedge as if compelled.

Nat watched them, and he watched the sea-birds too. Down in the bay they waited for the tide. They had more patience. Oyster-catchers, redshank, sanderling, and curlew watched by the water's edge; as the slow sea sucked at the shore and then withdrew, leaving the strip of seaweed bare and the shingle churned, the sea-birds raced and ran upon the beaches. Then that same impulse to flight seized upon them too. Crying, whistling, calling, they skimmed the placid sea and left the shore. Make haste, make speed, hurry and begone: yet where, and to what purpose? The restless urge of autumn, unsatisfying, sad, had put a spell upon them and they must flock, and wheel, and cry; they must spill themselves of motion before winter came.

Perhaps, thought Nat, munching his pasty by the cliff's edge, a message comes to the birds in autumn, like a warning. Winter is coming. Many of them perish. And like people who, apprehensive of death before their time, drive themselves to work or folly, the birds do likewise.

The birds had been more restless than ever this fall of the year, the agitation more marked because the days were still. As the tractor traced its path up and down the western hills, the figure of the farmer silhouetted on the driving-seat, the whole machine and the man upon it would be lost momentarily in the great cloud of wheeling, crying birds. There were many more than usual, Nat was sure of this. Always, in autumn, they followed the plough, but not in great flocks like these, nor with such clamour.

Nat remarked upon it, when hedging was finished for the day. 'Yes,' said the farmer, 'there are more birds about than usual; I've noticed it too. And daring, some of them, taking no notice of the tractor. One or two gulls came so close to my head this afternoon I thought they'd knock my cap off! As it was, I could scarcely see what I was doing, when they were overhead and I had the sun in my eyes. I have a notion the weather will change. It will be a hard winter. That's why the birds are restless.'

Nat, tramping home across the fields and down the lane to his cottage, saw the birds still flocking over the western hills, in the last glow of the sun. No wind, and the grey sea calm and full. Campion in bloom yet in the hedges, and the air mild. The farmer was right, though, and it was that night the weather turned. Nat's bedroom faced east. He woke just after two and heard the wind in the chimney. Not the storm and bluster of a sou'westerly gale, bringing the rain, but east wind, cold and dry. It sounded hollow in the chimney, and a loose slate rattled on the roof. Nat listened, and he coud hear the sea roaring in the bay. Even the air in the small bedroom had turned chill: a draught came under the skirting of the door, blowing upon the bed. Nat drew the blanket round him, leant closer to the back of his sleeping wife, and stayed wakeful, watchful, aware of misgiving without cause.

Then he heard the tapping on the window. There was no creeper on the cottage walls to break loose and scratch upon the pane. He listened, and the tapping continued until, irritated by the sound, Nat got out of bed and went to the window. He opened it, and as he did so something brushed his hand, jabbing at his knuckles, grazing the skin. Then he saw the flutter of the wings and it was gone, over the roof, behind the cottage.

It was a bird, what kind of bird he could not tell. The wind must have driven it to shelter on the sill.

He shut the window and went back to bed, but feeling his knuckles wet put his mouth to the scratch. The bird had drawn blood. Frightened, he supposed, and bewildered, the bird, seeking shelter, had stabbed at him in the darkness. Once more he settled himself to sleep.

Presently the tapping came again, this time more forceful, more insistent, and now his wife woke at the sound, and turning in the bed said to him, 'See to the window, Nat, it's rattling.'

'I've already seen to it,' he told her, 'there's some bird there, trying to get in. Can't you hear the wind? It's blowing from the east, driving the birds to shelter.'

'Send them away,' she said, 'I can't sleep with that noise.'

He went to the window for the second time, and now when he opened it there was not one bird upon the sill but half a dozen; they flew straight into his face, attacking him.

He shouted, striking out at them with his arms, scattering them; like the first one, they flew over the roof and disappeared. Quickly he let the window fall and latched it.

'Did you hear that?' he said. 'They went for me. Tried to peck my eyes.' He stood by the window, peering into the darkness, and could see nothing. His wife, heavy with sleep, murmured from the bed.

'I'm not making it up,' he said, angry at her suggestion. 'I tell you the birds were on the sill, trying to get into the room.'

Suddenly a frightened cry came from the room across the passage where the children slept.

'It's Jill,' said his wife, roused at the sound, sitting up in bed. 'Go to her, see what's the matter.'

Nat lit the candle, but when he opened the bedroom door to cross the passage the draught blew out the flame.

There came a second cry of terror, this time from both children, and stumbling into their room he felt the beating of wings about him in the darkness. The window was wide open. Through it came the birds, hitting first the ceiling and the walls, then swerving in mid-flight, turning to the children in their beds.

'It's all right, I'm here,' shouted Nat, and the children flung themselves, screaming, upon him, while in the darkness the birds rose and dived and came for him again.

'What is it, Nat, what's happened?' his wife called from the further bedroom, and swiftly he pushed the children through the door to the passage and shut it upon them, so that he was alone now, in their bedroom, with the birds.

He seized a blanket from the nearest bed, and using it as a weapon flung it to right and left about him in the air. He felt the thud of bodies, heard the fluttering of wings, but they were not yet defeated, for again and again they returned to the assault, jabbing his hands, his head, the little stabbing beaks sharp as a pointed fork. The blanket became a weapon of defence; he wound it about his head, and then in greater darkness beat at the birds with his bare hands. He dared not stumble to the door and open it, lest in doing so the birds should follow him.

How long he fought with them in the darkness he could not tell, but at last the beating of the wings about him lessened and then withdrew, and through the density of the blanket he was aware of light. He waited, listened; there was no sound except the fretful crying of one of the children from the bedroom beyond. The fluttering, the whirring of the wings had ceased.

He took the blanket from his head and stared about him. The cold grey morning light exposed the room. Dawn, and the open window, had called the living birds; the dead lay on the floor. Nat gazed at the little corpses, shocked and horrified. They were all small birds, none of any size; there must have been fifty of them lying there upon the floor. There were robins, finches, sparrows, blue tits, larks and bramblings, birds that by nature's law kept to their own flock and their own territory, and now, joining one with another in their urge for battle, had destroyed themselves against the bedroom walls, or in the strife had been destroyed by him. Some had lost feathers in the fight, others had blood, his blood, upon their beaks.

Sickened, Nat went to the window and stared out across his patch of garden to the fields.

It was bitter cold, and the ground had all the hard black look of frost. Not white frost, to shine in the morning sun, but the black frost that the east wind brings. The sea, fiercer now with the turning tide, white-capped and steep, broke harshly in the bay. Of the birds there was no sign. Not a sparrow chattered in the hedge beyond the garden gate, no early missel-thrush or blackbird pecked on the grass for worms. There was no sound at all but the east wind and the sea.

Nat shut the window and the door of the small bedroom, and went back across the passage to his own. His wife sat up in bed, one child asleep beside her, the smaller in her arms, his face bandaged. The curtains were tightly drawn across the window, the candles lit. Her face looked garish in the yellow light. She shook her head for silence.

'He's sleeping now,' she whispered, 'but only just. Something must have cut him, there was blood at the corner of his eyes. Jill said it was the birds. She said she woke up, and the birds were in the room.'

His wife looked up at Nat, searching his face for confirmation. She looked terrified, bewildered, and he

44

did not want her to know that he was also shaken, dazed almost, by the events of the past few hours.

'There are birds in there,' he said, 'dead birds, nearly fifty of them. Robins, wrens, all the little birds from hereabouts. It's as though a madness seized them, with the east wind.' He sat down on the bed beside his wife, and held her hand. 'It's the weather,' he said, 'it must be that, it's the hard weather. They aren't the birds, maybe, from here around. They've been driven down, from up country.'

'But Nat,' whispered his wife, 'it's only this night that the weather turned. There's been no snow to drive them. And they can't be hungry yet. There's food for them, out there, in the fields.'

'It's the weather,' repeated Nat. 'I tell you, it's the weather.'

His face too was drawn and tired, like hers. They stared at one another for a while without speaking.

'I'll go downstairs and make a cup of tea,' he said.

The sight of the kitchen reassured him. The cups and saucers, neatly stacked upon the dresser, the table and chairs, his wife's roll of knitting on her basket chair, the children's toys in a corner cupboard.

He knelt down, raked out the old embers and relit the fire. The glowing sticks brought normality, the steaming kettle and the brown teapot comfort and security. He drank his tea, carried a cup up to his wife. Then he washed in the scullery, and, putting on his boots, opened the back door.

The sky was hard and leaden, and the brown hills

that had gleamed in the sun the day before looked dark and bare. The east wind, like a razor, stripped the trees, and the leaves, crackling and dry, shivered and scattered with the wind's blast. Nat stubbed the earth with his boot. It was frozen hard. He had never known a change so swift and sudden. Black winter had descended in a single night.

The children were awake now. Jill was chattering upstairs and young Johnny crying once again. Nat heard his wife's voice, soothing, comforting. Presently they came down. He had breakfast ready for them, and the routine of the day began.

'Did you drive away the birds?' asked Jill, restored to calm because of the kitchen fire, because of day, because of breakfast.

'Yes, they've all gone now,' said Nat. 'It was the east wind brought them in. They were frightened and lost, they wanted shelter.'

'They tried to peck us,' said Jill. 'They went for Johnny's eyes.'

'Fright made them do that,' said Nat. 'They didn't know where they were, in the dark bedroom.'

'I hope they won't come again,' said Jill. 'Perhaps if we put bread for them outside the window they will eat that and fly away.'

She finished her breakfast and then went for her coat and hood, her school books and her satchel. Nat said nothing, but his wife looked at him across the table. A silent message passed between them.

46

'I'll walk with her to the bus,' he said, 'I don't go to the farm today.'

And while the child was washing in the scullery he said to his wife, 'Keep all the windows closed, and the doors too. Just to be on the safe side. I'll go to the farm. Find out if they heard anything in the night.' Then he walked with his small daughter up the lane. She seemed to have forgotten her experience of the night before. She danced ahead of him, chasing the leaves, her face whipped with the cold and rosy under the pixie hood.

'Is it going to snow, Dad?' she said. 'It's cold enough.'

He glanced up at the bleak sky, felt the wind tear at his shoulders.

'No,' he said, 'it's not going to snow. This is a black winter, not a white one.'

All the while he searched the hedgerows for the birds, glanced over the top of them to the fields beyond, looked to the small wood above the farm where the rooks and jackdaws gathered. He saw none.

The other children waited by the bus-stop, muffled, hooded like Jill, the faces white and pinched with cold.

Jill ran to them, waving. 'My Dad says it won't snow,' she called, 'it's going to be a black winter.'

She said nothing of the birds. She began to push and struggle with another little girl. The bus came ambling up the hill. Nat saw her on to it, then turned and walked back towards the farm. It was not his day for work, but he wanted to satisfy himself that all was well. Jim, the cowman, was clattering in the yard.

'Boss around?' asked Nat.

'Gone to market,' said Jim. 'It's Tuesday, isn't it?'

He clumped off round the corner of a shed. He had no time for Nat. Nat was said to be superior. Read books, and the like. Nat had forgotten it was Tuesday. This showed how the events of the preceding night had shaken him. He went to the back door of the farm-house and heard Mrs Trigg singing in the kitchen, the wireless making a background to her song.

'Are you there, missus?' called out Nat.

She came to the door, beaming, broad, a good-tempered woman.

'Hullo, Mr Hocken,' she said. 'Can you tell me where this cold is coming from? Is it Russia? I've never seen such a change. And it's going on, the wireless says. Something to do with the Arctic circle.'

'We didn't turn on the wireless this morning,' said Nat. 'Fact is, we had trouble in the night.'

'Kiddies poorly?'

'No . . .' He hardly knew how to explain it. Now, in daylight, the battle of the birds would sound absurd.

He tried to tell Mrs Trigg what had happened, but he could see from her eyes that she thought his story was the result of a nightmare.

'Sure they were real birds,' she said, smiling, 'with proper feathers and all? Not the funny-shaped kind, that the men see after closing hours on a Saturday night?'

'Mrs Trigg,' he said, 'there are fifty dead birds, robins, wrens, and such, lying low on the floor of the children's bedroom. They went for me; they tried to go for young Johnny's eyes.'

48

Mrs Trigg stared at him doubtfully.

'Well there, now,' she answered, 'I suppose the weather brought them. Once in the bedroom, they wouldn't know where they were to. Foreign birds maybe, from that Arctic circle.'

'No,' said Nat, 'they were the birds you see about here every day.'

'Funny thing,' said Mrs Trigg, 'no explaining it, really. You ought to write up and ask the *Guardian*. They'd have some answer for it. Well, I must be getting on.'

She nodded, smiled, and went back into the kitchen.

Nat, dissatisfied, turned to the farm-gate. Had it not been for those corpses on the bedroom floor, which he must now collect and bury somewhere, he would have considered the tale exaggeration too.

Jim was standing by the gate.

'Had any trouble with the birds?' asked Nat.

'Birds? What birds?'

'We got them up our place last night. Scores of them, came in the children's bedroom. Quite savage they were.'

'Oh?' It took time for anything to penetrate Jim's head. 'Never heard of birds acting savage,' he said at length. 'They get tame, like, sometimes. I've seen them come to the windows for crumbs.'

'These birds last night weren't tame.'

'No? Cold maybe. Hungry. You put out some crumbs.'

Jim was no more interested than Mrs Trigg had been. It was, Nat thought, like air-raids in the war. No one down this end of the country knew what the Plymouth folk had seen and suffered. You had to endure something yourself before it touched you. He walked back along the lane and crossed the stile to his cottage. He found his wife in the kitchen with young Johnny.

'See anyone?' she asked.

'Mrs Trigg and Jim,' he answered. 'I don't think they believed me. Anyway, nothing wrong up there.'

'You might take the birds away,' she said. 'I daren't go into the room to make the beds until you do. I'm scared.'

'Nothing to scare you now,' said Nat. 'They're dead, aren't they?'

He went up with a sack and dropped the stiff bodies into it, one by one. Yes, there were fifty of them, all told. Just the ordinary common birds of the hedgerow, nothing as large even as a thrush. It must have been fright that made them act the way they did. Blue tits, wrens, it was incredible to think of the power of their small beaks, jabbing at his face and hands the night before. He took the sack out into the garden and was faced now with a fresh problem. The ground was too hard to dig. It was frozen solid, yet no snow had fallen, nothing had happened in the past hours but the coming of the east wind. It was unnatural, queer. The weather prophets must be right. The change was something connected with the Arctic circle.

The wind seemed to cut him to the bone as he stood there, uncertainly, holding the sack. He could see the white-capped seas breaking down under in the bay. He decided to take the birds to the shore and bury them.

When he reached the beach below the headland he could scarcely stand, the force of the east wind was so strong. It hurt to draw breath, and his bare hands were blue. Never had he known such cold, not in all the bad winters he could remember. It was low tide. He crunched his way over the shingle to the softer sand and then, his back to the wind, ground a pit in the sand with his heel. He meant to drop the birds into it, but as he opened up the sack the force of the wind carried them, lifted them, as though in flight again, and they were blown away from him along the beach, tossed like feathers, spread and scattered, the bodies of the fifty frozen birds. There was something ugly in the sight. He did not like it. The dead birds were swept away from him by the wind.

'The tide will take them when it turns,' he said to himself.

He looked out to sea and watched the crested breakers, combing green. They rose stiffly, curled, and broke again, and because it was ebb tide the roar was distant, more remote, lacking the sound and thunder of the flood.

Then he saw them. The gulls. Out there, riding the seas.

What he had thought at first to be the white caps of the waves were gulls. Hundreds, thousands, tens of thousand . . . They rose and fell in the trough of the seas, heads to the wind, like a mighty fleet at anchor, waiting on the tide. To eastward, and to the west, the gulls were there. They stretched as far as his eye could reach, in close formation, line upon line. Had the sea been still they would have covered the bay like a white cloud, head to head, body packed to body. Only the east wind, whipping the sea to breakers, hid them from the shore.

Nat turned, and leaving the beach climbed the steep path home. Someone should know of this. Someone should be told. Something was happening, because of the east wind and the weather, that he did not understand. He wondered if he should go to the call-box by the bus-stop and ring up the police. Yet what could they do? What could anyone do? Tens and thousands of gulls riding the sea there, in the bay, because of storm, because of hunger. The police would think him mad, or drunk, or take the statement from him with great calm. 'Thank you. Yes, the matter has already been reported. The hard weather is driving the birds inland in great numbers.' Nat looked about him. Still no sign of any other bird. Perhaps the cold had sent them all from up country? As he drew near to the cottage his wife came to meet him, at the door. She called to him, excited. 'Nat,' she said, 'it's on the wireless. They've just read out a special news bulletin. I've written it down.'

'What's on the wireless?' he said.

'About the birds,' she said. 'It's not only here, it's everywhere. In London, all over the country. Something has happened to the birds.'

Together they went into the kitchen. He read the piece of paper lying on the table.

'Statement from the Home Office at eleven a.m. today. Reports from all over the country are coming in hourly about the vast quantity of birds flocking above towns, villages, and outlying districts, causing obstruction and damage and even attacking individuals. It is thought that the Arctic air stream, at present covering the British Isles, is causing birds to migrate south in immense numbers, and that intense hunger may drive these birds to attack human beings. Householders are warned to see to their windows, doors, and chimneys, and to take reasonable precautions for the safety of their children. A further statement will be issued later.'

A kind of excitement seized Nat; he looked at his wife in triumph.

'There you are,' he said, 'let's hope they'll hear that at the farm. Mrs Trigg will know it wasn't any story. It's true. All over the country. I've been telling myself all morning there's something wrong. And just now, down on the beach, I looked out to sea and there are gulls, thousands of them, tens of thousands, you couldn't put a pin between their heads, and they're all out there, riding on the sea, waiting.'

'What are they waiting for, Nat?' she asked.

He stared at her, then looked down again at the piece of paper.

'I don't know,' he said slowly. 'It says here the birds are hungry.'

He went over to the drawer where he kept his hammer and tools.

'What are you going to do, Nat?'

'See to the windows and the chimneys too, like they tell you.'

'You think they would break in, with the windows shut? Those sparrows and robins and such? Why, how could they?'

He did not answer. He was not thinking of the robins and the sparrows. He was thinking of the gulls . . .

He went upstairs and worked there the rest of the morning, boarding the windows of the bedrooms, filling up the chimney bases. Good job it was his free day and he was not working at the farm. It reminded him of the old days, at the beginning of the war. He was not married then, and he had made all the blackout boards for his mother's house in Plymouth. Made the shelter too. Not that it had been of any use, when the moment came. He wondered if they would take these precautions up at the farm. He doubted it. Too easy-going, Harry Trigg and his missus. Maybe they'd laugh at the whole thing. Go off to a dance or a whist drive.

'Dinner's ready.' She called him, from the kitchen.

'All right. Coming down.'

He was pleased with his handiwork. The frames fitted nicely over the little panes and at the base of the chimneys.

When dinner was over and his wife was washing up, Nat switched on the one o'clock news. The same announcement was repeated, the one which she had taken down during the morning, but the news bulletin enlarged upon it. 'The flocks of birds have caused dislocation in all areas,' read the announcer, 'and in London the sky was so dense at ten o'clock this morning that it seemed as if the city was covered by a vast black cloud.

'The birds settled on roof-tops, on window ledges and on chimneys. The species included blackbird, thrush, the common house-sparrow, and, as might be expected in the metropolis, a vast quantity of pigeons and starlings, and that frequenter of the London river, the black-headed gull. The sight has been so unusual that traffic came to a standstill in many thoroughfares, work was abandoned in shops and offices, and the streets and pavements were crowded with people standing about to watch the birds.'

Various incidents were recounted, the suspected reason of cold and hunger stated again, and warnings to householders repeated. The announcer's voice was smooth and suave. Nat had the impression that this man, in particular, treated the whole business as he would an elaborate joke. There would be others like him, hundreds of them, who did not know what it was to struggle in darkness with a flock of birds. There would be parties tonight in London, like the ones they gave on election nights. People standing about, shouting and laughing, getting drunk. 'Come and watch the birds!'

Nat switched off the wireless. He got up and started work on the kitchen windows. His wife watched him, young Johnny at her heels.

'What, boards for down here too?' she said. 'Why, I'll have to light up before three o'clock. I see no call for boards down here.'

'Better be sure than sorry,' answered Nat. 'I'm not going to take any chances.'

'What they ought to do,' she said, 'is to call the army out and shoot the birds. That would soon scare them off.'

'Let them try,' said Nat. 'How'd they set about it?'

'They have the army to the docks,' she answered, 'when the dockers strike. The soldiers go down and unload the ships.'

'Yes,' said Nat, 'and the population of London is eight million or more. Think of all the buildings, all the flats, and houses. Do you think they've enough soldiers to go round shooting birds from every roof?'

'I don't know. But something should be done. They ought to do something.'

Nat thought to himself that 'they' were no doubt considering the problem at that very moment, but whatever 'they' decided to do in London and the big cities would not help the people here, three hundred miles away. Each householder must look after his own.

'How are we off for food?' he said.

'Now, Nat, whatever next?'

'Never mind. What have you got in the larder?'

'It's shopping day tomorrow, you know that. I don't keep uncooked food hanging about, it goes off. Butcher doesn't call till the day after. But I can bring back something when I go in tomorrow.'

Nat did not want to scare her. He thought it possible that she might not go to town tomorrow. He looked in the larder for himself, and in the cupboard where she kept her tins. They would do, for a couple of days. Bread was low.

'What about the baker?'

'He comes tomorrow too.'

He saw she had flour. If the baker did not call she had enough to bake one loaf.

'We'd be better off in the old days,' he said, 'when the women baked twice a week, and had pilchards salted, and there was food for a family to last a siege, if need be.'

'I've tried the children with tinned fish, they don't like it,' she said.

Nat went on hammering the boards across the kitchen windows. Candles. They were low in candles too. That must be another thing she meant to buy tomorrow. Well, it could not be helped. They must go early to bed tonight. That was, if . . .

He got up and went out of the back door and stood in the garden, looking down towards the sea. There had been no sun all day, and now, at barely three o'clock, a kind of darkness had already come, the sky sullen, heavy, colourless like salt. He could hear the vicious sea drumming on the rocks. He walked down the path, half-way to the beach. And then he stopped. He could see the tide had turned. The rock that had shown in mid-morning was now covered, but it was not the sea that held his eyes. The gulls had risen. They were circling, hundreds of them, thousands of them, lifting their wings against the wind. It was the gulls that made the darkening of the sky. And they were silent. They made not a sound. They just went on soaring and circling, rising, falling, trying their strength against the wind.

Nat turned. He ran up the path, back to the cottage.

'I'm going for Jill,' he said. 'I'll wait for her, at the bus-stop.'

'What's the matter?' asked his wife. 'You've gone quite white.'

'Keep Johnny inside,' he said. 'Keep the door shut. Light up now, and draw the curtains.'

'It's only just gone three,' she said.

'Never mind. Do what I tell you.'

He looked inside the toolshed, outside the back door. Nothing there of much use. A spade was too heavy, and a fork no good. He took the hoe. It was the only possible tool, and light enough to carry.

He started walking up the lane to the bus-stop, and now and again glanced back over his shoulder.

The gulls had risen higher now, their circles were broader, wider, they were spreading out in huge formation across the sky.

He hurried on; although he knew the bus would not come to the top of the hill before four o'clock he had to hurry. He passed no one on the way. He was glad of this. No time to stop and chatter.

At the top of the hill he waited. He was much too soon. There was half an hour still to go. The east wind came whipping across the fields from the higher ground. He stamped his feet and blew upon his hands. In the distance he could see the clay hills, white and clean, against the heavy pallor of the sky. Something black rose from behind them, like a smudge at first, then widening, becoming deeper, and the smudge became a cloud, and the cloud divided again into five other clouds, spreading north, east, south and west, and they were not clouds at all; they were birds. He watched them travel across the sky, and as one section passed overhead, within two or three hundred feet of him, he knew from their speed, they were bound inland, up country, they had no business with the people here on the peninsula. They were rooks, crows, jackdaws, magpies, jays, all birds that usually preyed upon the smaller species; but this afternoon they were bound on some other mission.

'They've been given the towns,' thought Nat, 'they know what they have to do. We don't matter so much here. The gulls will serve for us. The others go to the towns.'

He went to the call-box, stepped inside and lifted the receiver. The exchange would do. They would pass the message on.

'I'm speaking from Highway,' he said, 'by the bus-stop. I want to report large formations of birds travelling up country. The gulls are also forming in the bay.'

'All right,' answered the voice, laconic, weary.

'You'll be sure and pass this message on to the proper quarter?'

'Yes . . . yes . . .' Impatient now, fed-up. The buzzing note resumed.

'She's another,' thought Nat, 'she doesn't care. Maybe she's had to answer calls all day. She hopes to go to the pictures tonight. She'll squeeze some fellow's hand, and point up at the sky, and say "Look at all them birds!" She doesn't care.'

The bus came lumbering up the hill. Jill climbed out and three or four other children. The bus went on towards the town.

'What's the hoe for, Dad?'

They crowded around him, laughing, pointing.

'I just brought it along,' he said. 'Come on now, let's get home. It's cold, no hanging about. Here, you. I'll watch you across the fields, see how fast you can run.'

He was speaking to Jill's companions who came from different families, living in the council houses. A short cut would take them to the cottages.

'We want to play a bit in the lane,' said one of them.

'No, you don't. You go off home, or I'll tell your mammy.'

They whispered to one another, round-eyed, then scuttled off across the fields. Jill stared at her father, her mouth sullen.

'We always play in the lane,' she said.

'Not tonight, you don't,' he said. 'Come on now, no dawdling.'

He could see the gulls now, circling the fields, coming in towards the land. Still silent. Still no sound.

'Look, Dad, look over there, look at all the gulls.'

'Yes. Hurry, now.'

'Where are they flying to? Where are they going?'

'Up country, I dare say. Where it's warmer.'

He seized her hand and dragged her after him along the lane.

'Don't go so fast. I can't keep up.'

The gulls were copying the rooks and crows. They were spreading out in formation across the sky. They headed, in bands of thousands, to the four compass points.

'Dad, what is it?'

ARTHUR QUILLER-COUCH
(1863–1944)

While we're in Fowey, let's wander along the Esplanade and pay a visit to that dapper old gent Sir Arthur Quiller-Couch, or 'Q' as he was called. You'd know him if you saw him. Q was a snazzy dresser and the inspiration for Ratty in Kenneth Grahame's *The Wind in the Willows*, and loved nothing better than 'messing around in boats' here on the Fowey, sometimes with friends like Grahame, J. M. Barrie or the du Mauriers.

Q was known for his *Oxford Book of English Verse* and the series of lectures from his fellowship at Jesus College, Cambridge, collected as *The Art of Writing*. (The latter includes the creative writing mantra 'Murder your darlings', a piece of editing advice that would later be misattributed to William Faulkner.) But as well as these more serious works, Q was a writer of adventure, his novels filled with buccaneers, romance and the supernatural, with titles like *Poison Island* and *Dead Man's Rock*.

Poison Island is a story in the manner of R. L. Stevenson, whom Q admired greatly. It has an old sea captain, a murder and pirate treasure, with evocatively named characters such as Captain Coffin, Miss Belcher and Dr Beauregard. There's even a treasure map of an island where X marks the spot. The adventure begins in Falmouth town, with young Harry Brooks on his way to see the captain.

from Poison Island

A barber's pole protruded beside the ope leading to Captain Coffin's lodgings. It was painted in spirals of scarlet and blue, and at the end of it a cage containing a grey parrot dangled over the footway.

"Drunk again!" screamed the parrot, as I hesitated before the entrance, for the directing-marks just here were so numerous as to be perplexing. To the right of the alley the barber had affixed his signboard, close above the base of his pole; to the left a flanking slopshop dangled a row of cast-off suits, while immediately overhead was nailed a board painted over with ornate flourishes and the legend—

"G. Goodfellow. Carpenter and House-Decorator, &c. Repairs Neatly Executed. Instruction in the Violin. Funerals at the Shortest Notice. Shipping Supplied."

"Drunk again!" repeated the parrot. "Kiss me, kiss me, kiss me, kiss me! Oh, you nasty image! Kiss me, kiss me! Who killed the Portugee?"

"He don't mean you," explained the barber, reassuringly, emerging at that moment from his shop with a pannikin of water for the parrot's cage, which he lowered very deftly by means of a halliard reeved through a block at the end of the pole. "He means old Coffin. Nice bird, hey?"

He slipped a hand through the cage-door, and caressed him, scratching his head.

"If you please, sir," said I, "it's Captain Coffin I'm looking for."

"Drunk again!" screamed the bird. "Damn my giblets, drunk again!"

"He don't like Coffin, and that's a fact," said the barber.

"He don't appear to, sir," I agreed.

"You'll find the old fellow down the yard. That is, if you really want him." The barber eyed me doubtfully. "He's sober enough, just now; been swearin' off liquor for a week. I dare say you know his temper's uncertain at such times."

I did not know it, but was too far committed to retreat.

"Well, you'll find him down the yard—green door to the right, with the brass knocker. He's out at the back, hammering at his ship, but he'll hear you fast enough: he's wonderful quick of hearing."

A man, even though he possessed a solid brass knocker, had need to be quick of hearing in that alley. Without, street-hawkers were bawling and carts rattling on the cobbled thoroughfare; from the entrance the parrot vociferated after me as I went down the passage beneath an open window whence an invisible violin repeated the opening phrase of "Come, cheer up, my lads!" plaintively and persistently; while from the far end, somewhere between it and the harbour side, an irregular hammering punctuated the music.

I knocked, and the hammering ceased. The rest of the din ceased not, nor abated. In about a minute the green door opened—a cautious inch or two at first, then wide enough to reveal Captain Coffin. He wore a dirty white jumper over his upper garments, and held a formidable mallet. I observed that either his face was unnaturally white or the rims of his eyes were unnaturally red, and that sawdust be-sprinkled his hair and collar. I recalled the tavern sawdust which had bepowdered his hat on the night of our first meeting, and jumped to a wrong conclusion.

"Eh? It's Brooks—the boy Brooks! Glad to see you, Brooks! Come inside."

"Thank you, sir," said I, feeling a strong impulse to bolt as he shook me by the hand, so hot was his and so dry, and so feverishly it gripped me.

"You're sure no one tracked ye here?" he asked, as he closed the door behind us.

"There was a barber, sir, at the head of the passage. I stopped to ask him the way."

"*He's* all right, or would be but for that cursed bird of his. How a man can keep such a bird—" Captain Coffin broke off. "I had a two-three nails in my mouth when you knocked. Nearly made me swallow 'em, you did. They was copper nails, too."

I suppose I must have stared at this, for he paused and peered at me, drawing me over to the window, through which—so thickly grimed it was—a very little light dribbled from the courtyard into the room. Yet the room itself was clean, almost spick and span, with a seaman-like tidiness in all its arrangements—a small room, crowded with foreign odds-and-ends, among which I remember a walking-stick even more singular than the one Captain Coffin carried on his walks abroad (it was white in colour, with lines of small grey indentations, and he afterwards told me it was a shark's backbone); a corner-cupboard, too, painted over with green-and-yellow tulips.

"Copper nails, I tell you. Nothing but the best'll do for your friend Coffin." He leaned back, still eyeing me, and tapped me twice on the chest. "You heard me say that? 'Your friend' was my words."

"Thank you, sir."

"But you made me jump, you did—me being that way given when off the liquor." He hesitated a moment, with a glance over his shoulder at the tulip-painted cupboard. "Brooks," he went on earnestly, "you and me being met on a matter of business, and the same needin' steadiness—head and hand, my boy, if ever business did—what d'ye say to a tot of rum apiece?"

Without waiting for my answer, he hobbled off to the cupboard, and had set two glasses on the table and brimmed them with neat spirit before I had finished protesting. The bottle-neck trembled on the rims of the glasses and struck out a sort of chime as he paused.

"You won't?" he asked, gulping down his own portion; and the liquor must have been potent, for it brought a sudden water to his eyes. "Well, so be it—if you've kept off it at your age. But at mine"—he drank off the second glassful and wiped his mouth—"I've had experiences, Brooks. When you've heard 'em, you wouldn't be surprised, not if it took a dozen to steady me."

He filled again, and came close to me, holding the glass, yet so tremulously that the rum spilled over his fingers.

"Ingots, lad—golden ingots! Bars and wedges of solid gold! Gems, too, and cath-e-deral plate, with crucifixions and priests' vestments stiff with pearls and rubies as if they was frozen. I've seen 'em lyin' tossed in a heap like mullet in a ground-net. Ay, and blazin' on the beach, with the gulls screamin' over 'em and flappin', and the sea all around. I seen it with these eyes, boy!" He stood back and shivered. "And behind o' that, the Death! But it comes equal to all, the Death. Not if a man had learned every trick the devil can teach could he lay his course clear o' that. Could he, now?"

His words, his uncouth gestures, which were almost spasms, and the changes in his face—from cupidity to terror, and from terror again to a kind of wistful hope—fairly frightened me, and I stammered stupidly that death was the common lot, and there couldn't be a doubt of it; that or something of the sort. But what I said does not matter. He was not listening, and before I had done he drained and set down the glass and gripped my arm again.

"I seen all that—ay, an' felt it!" He drew away and stretched out both hands, crooking his fingers like talons. "Ay, an' I seen *him!*"

"Him?" I echoed. "But you were talking of Death, sir."

"You may call him that. There's men lyin' around in the sand—Did ever you hear, boy, of a poison that kills a man and keeps him fresh as paint?"

"No, sir."

He nodded. "No, I reckon you never did. Fresh as paint it keeps 'em, and white as a figurehead. The first heap as ever I dug, believin' it to be the treasure—my reckoning was out by a foot or two—I came on one o' them. Three foot beneath the sand I came on him, an' the gulls sheevoing all the while over my head. *They* knew. And the sea and the dreadful loneliness around us all the while. There was three of us, Brooks—I mention no names, you understand—three of us, and *him*. Three to one. Yet he got the better of us all—as he got the better of the first lot, and *they* must ha' been a dozen. Four of them we uncovered afore we struck the edge of the treasure—uncovered 'em and covered 'em up again pretty quick, I can tell you. Fresh as paint they were, in a manner o' speaking, just as though they'd died yesterday; where*as* by Bill's account they must ha' lain there for more'n a year. And the faces on 'em white and shinin'—"

Here Captain Coffin shivered, and, glancing about him, poured out another go of rum.

"You wouldn't blame me for wantin' it, Brooks—not if you'd seen 'em. That was on the Keys, as they're called—half a dozen banks to no'thard of the island, and maybe from half a mile to three-quarters off the shore, which shoals thereabout—sand, all the lot of 'em, and nothin' but sand; sand and sea-birds, and—what I told you. But the bulk lies in the island itself, in two caches; and where the bigger cache lies *he* don't know, and nobody knows but only Dan Coffin."

Captain Coffin winked, touched his breast, and wagged his forefinger at me impressively.

"That makes twice," he went on. "Twice that devil has got the better of every one. But the third time's lucky, they say. He may be dead afore this; he'll be getting an oldish man, anyway, and life on that cursed island can't be good for his health. We won't go in a crowd this time, neither; not a dozen, nor yet four of us, but only you an' me, Brooks. It's the safer way—the only safe way—an' there'll be the fatter sharin's. Now you know—hey?—why Branscome's givin' me lessons in navigation."

He chuckled, and was moving off mysteriously to a back doorway behind the dresser, but halted and came back to the table beside which I stood, making no motion to follow him.

"Look ye here, Brooks," said he. "If there's anything you don't get the hang of—anything that takes ye aback, so to speak, in what I'm tellin' you—you just hitch on an' trust to old Dan Coffin; to old Dan, as'll do for you more than ever your godfathers an' godmothers did at your baptism. You'll pick up a full breeze as you go on. Man, the treasure's there! Man, I've handled it, or enough of it to keep you in a coach-an'-six, with nothing to do but loll on cushions for the rest o' your days, an' pick your teeth at the crowd. And look ye here." He waved a hand around the room. "I'm old Danny Coffin, ain't I? poor old drunken Danny Coffin, eh? Yet cast an eye about ye. Nice fittin's, ben't they? Hitch down my coat off the peg there; feel the cloth of it; take it between finger and thumb. Ay, I don't live upon air, nor keep house an' fixtures upon nothin' at all. There—if you want more proof!" He dived a hand into his trouser-pocket, and held out a golden coin under my nose. "There! that very dollar came from the island, and I'm offerin' you the fellows to it by the thousand. Why? says you. Because, says I, you're a good lad, and I've took a fancy to see you in Parlyment. That's why. An' it's no return I'm askin' you, but just to believe!"

He made for the back door again, and opened it, letting in the sunlight; but the sunlight fell in two slanting rays, one on either side of a dark object which all but filled the entrance, blocking out my view of the back court beyond. It was the stern of a tall boat.

GOTTFRIED VON STRASSBURG
(died *c.* 1210)

Tristan was one of the greatest knights of Arthurian legend, and while Arthur himself has been claimed by Wales, Glastonbury and a handful of other locations, the tragedy of Tristan is a thoroughly Cornish one.

The hero is sent by his uncle, King Mark of Cornwall, to fetch the beautiful Iseult of Ireland, whom Mark was to wed so that the war between Cornwall and Ireland might be ended. King Mark's castle is said to be just above Fowey, at Castledore.

On the ship back to Cornwall Iseult and Tristan fell in love, largely thanks to a magic potion they accidentally drank. Their love is in turn illicit, funny, magnificent, and ultimately tragic.

In the following section Tristan and Iseult have been caught together again and King Mark has exiled them to the wilderness, which was not the terrible punishment he intended it to be . . .

from The Story of Tristan and Iseult
translated by Jessie L. Weston

Now, Tristan aforetime knew of a cave in a wild hill, which he had once chanced upon while hunting. This same cavern in the old days of heathendom, when giants were lords of the land, had been hewn by them in the hillside. 'Twas there they were wont to resort secretly for love-dalliance, and when any such were found they were shut in with brazen doors and named Love Grottoes.

The cavern was round, large, and lofty; the walls snow-white and smooth; the vault above bare in the centre, at the keystone, a crown richly wrought in metal work and adorned with gems; the floor below was of polished marble, its hue green as grass.

In the centre was a couch, carved out of a crystal stone, with letters engraven all around, saying 'twas dedicated to the Goddess of Love. High in the wall of the cavern were little windows hewn in the rock, through which the light might enter. Before the entrance was a brazen door, and without there stood three lindens and no more; but all around the hill and towards the valley were countless trees, whose boughs and foliage gave a fair shade. On one side was a little glade and a spring of water, cool and fresh and clear as sunlight, and above the spring were again three lindens, which sheltered it alike from sun and rain; and all over the glade the bright blossoms and green grass strove with each other for the mastery, each would fain overcome the brightness of the other.

In the branches the birds sang sweetly, so sweetly that nowhere else might one hear the like. Eye and ear alike found solace. There were shade and sunshine, air and soft breezes.

From this hill and this grotto for a good day's journey was there nought but rocks, waste and wild and void of game. Nor was the road smooth and easy, yet was it not so rough but that Tristan and his true love might make their way thither and find shelter in the hill.

Now when they had come to their journey's end, and thought to abide there, they sent Kurwenal back, bidding him say at the court that Tristan and Iseult, with much grief, had sailed thence to Ireland to make their innocence plain to all; and he had thought it best to return straightway to court. Then they bade him seek out Brangœne and give her tidings of her friends, and learn from her how it stood with King Mark, and if he had lent an ear to evil counsels, and purposed any treachery against the life of the lovers. He was thus to watch how matters went for Tristan and Iseult, and once in every twenty days bear them tidings from the court.

What more shall I say? Kurwenal did as he was bade, and Tristan and Iseult remained alone to make their dwelling in this wild hermitage.

Many have marvelled wherewith the twain might support their life in this wilderness, but in truth they needed little save each other, the true love and faith they bare the one to the other, such love as kindles the heart and refreshes the soul, that was their best nourishment. They asked but rarely for other than the food which giveth to the heart its desire, to the eyes their delight; therewith had they enough.

Nor did it vex them that they were thus alone in the wild woodland; what should they want with other company? They were there together, a third would but have made unequal what was equal, and oppressed that fellowship which was so fair. Even good King Arthur never held at his court a feast that might have brought them greater joy and refreshment. Search through all the lands, and ye might not have found a joy, however great, for which these twain would have bartered a glass finger ring.

They had a court, they had a council, which brought them nought but joy. Their courtiers were the green trees, the shade and the sunlight, the streamlet and the spring; flowers, grass, leaf and blossom, which refreshed their eyes. Their service was the song of the birds, the little brown nightingales, the throstles, and the merles; and other wood birds. The siskin and the ring-dove vied with each other to do them pleasure; all day long their music rejoiced ear and soul.

Their love was their high feast, which brought them a thousand times daily the joy of Arthur's Round Table and the fellowship of his knights. What might they ask better? The man was with the woman and the woman with the man, they had the fellowship they most desired, and were where they fain would be.

In the dewy morning they gat them forth to the meadow where grass and flowers alike had been refreshed. The glade was their pleasure ground—they wandered hither and thither, hearkening each other's speech and waking the song of the birds by their footsteps. Then they turned them to where the cold clear spring rippled forth, and sat beside its stream, and watched its flow till the sun grew high in heaven, and they felt its heat. Then they betook them to the linden: its branches offered them a welcome shelter, the breezes were sweet and soft beneath its shade, and the couch at its feet was decked with the fairest grass and flowers.

There they sat side by side, those true lovers, and told each other tales of those who ere their time had suffered and died for love. They mourned the fate of the sad Queen Dido; of Phyllis of Thrace; and Biblis, whose heart brake for love. With such tales did they beguile the time. But when they would think of them no more they turned them again to their grotto and took the harp, and each in their turn sang to it softly lays of love and of longing; now Tristan would strike the harp while Iseult sang the words, then it would be the turn of Iseult to make music while Tristan's voice followed the notes. Full well might it be called the Love Grotto.

At times they would ride forth with the crossbow to shoot the wild game of the woodland, or to chase the red deer with their hound Hiudan, for Tristan had taught him to hunt hart and hind silently, nor to give tongue when on their track. This would they do many days, yet more for the sake of sport and pleasure than to supply themselves with food, for in sooth they had no care save to do what might please them best at the moment.

While they thus dwelt in the woods, King Mark in his palace was but sorrowful, for he grieved ever for his honour and for his wife, and his heart grew heavier day by day.

In these days, more to solace himself than for love of adventure, he bethought him to ride forth to the chase, and by chance he came into that very wood where Tristan and Iseult had their dwelling. The huntsmen and their dogs came upon a herd of deer and separated a strange stag from among them. He was white, with a mane like to that of a horse, and larger than stags are wont to be. His horns were small and short, scarce grown, as if he had but lately shed them; and they chased this stag hotly till evening, but he fled from thence to the wood of the Grotto, whence he came, and thus escaped.

King Mark was greatly vexed, and the huntsman even more, that they had lost the quarry (for the beast was passing strange in form and colour), and they were all ill pleased. So they turned not homeward, but encamped in the wood for the night, thinking to take up the chase on the morrow.

Now, Tristan and Iseult had heard all day long the sound of the chase, for the wood rang with the horns and the baying of the hounds. They thought it could be no one but Mark, and their hearts grew heavy within them, for they deemed they were betrayed.

The next morning the chief huntsman arose ere the flush of dawn was in the sky; he bade his underlings wait till the day had fully broken and then follow him. In a leash he took a brachet, which served him well and led him on the right track. It guided him onwards through many rough places, over rocks and hard ground, through barren lands and over grass where yestereven the stag had fled before him. The huntsman followed straight on the track till at last the narrow path came to an end, and the sun shone out clearly; he was by the spring in Tristan's glade.

That same morning had Tristan and his lady love stolen forth, hand in hand, and come full early, through the morning dew, to the flowery meadow and the lovely vale. Dove and nightingale saluted them sweetly, greeting their friends Tristan and Iseult. The wild wood birds bade them welcome in their own tongue,—'twas as if they had conspired among themselves to give the lovers a morning greeting. They sang from the leafy branches in changeful wise, answering each other in song and refrain. The spring that charmed their eye and ear whispered a welcome, even as did the linden with its rustling leaves. The blossoming trees, the fair meadow, the flowers and the green grass, all that bloomed laughed at their coming; the dew which cooled their feet, and refreshed their heart, offered a silent greeting.

When the twain had rejoiced them enough in the fair morning air they betook them again to their grotto, fearing lest the hunt might come their way, and one of the hounds discover their hiding-place. After awhile they laid them down on the couch, apart, and Tristan laid his unsheathed sword between them—so they fell asleep.

Now, the huntsman of whom I spake but now, who had followed the trail of the stag to the spring, he spied in the morning dew the track left by Tristan and his lady, and he bethought him 'twas but the trial he was following. So he dismounted and followed, till he came to the door of the grotto; 'twas fastened with two bolts, so that he might go no further.

Marvelling much, he turned aside, and sought all around and over the hill, till by chance he found a little window, high up in the wall of the grotto. Fearing greatly he looked through, and saw nought but a man and a woman. Yet the sight moved him to wonder, for he thought that of a truth the woman came of no mortal race, none such had ever been born into this world. Yet he did not stay long at gaze, for he spied the unsheathed sword, and drew back in terror—he deemed that here was magic at work, and was affrighted to remain. So he made his way down the hill and rode back towards the hounds.

Now, King Mark had become aware that his chief huntsman had ridden forth after the stag, and had hastened to meet him.

"Sir King," said the huntsman, "I will tell thee a marvel; I have but now found a fair adventure!"

"Say, what adventure?"

"I have found a Love Grotto!"

"Where and how didst thou find it?"

"Sire, here, in this wilderness."

"What? Here, in this wild woodland?"

"Yea, even here."

"Is there any living soul within?"

"Sire, a man and a goddess are within. They lie side by side on a couch and seem to slumber. The man is even as other men, but I doubt me for his companion, if she be mortal! She is more beautiful than a fairy. Never was any so fair of mortal flesh. And between them lieth a sword, bare, bright, and keen. I know not what it may betoken."

The king quoth: "Lead me thither."

The master huntsman led him forthwith on the track of the game to the spot where he had dismounted. The king alighted on the grass, and followed the path the huntsman shewed him. So came King Mark to the door, and turned aside and climbed the hill even to the summit, making many a twist and turn as the huntsman had told him. And he, too, found at last the window and looked through, and saw the twain lie on the crystal couch, sleeping as before; and he saw them even as the huntsman had said, apart, with the naked sword blade between them, and knew them for his nephew and his wife.

His heart grew cold within him for sorrow, and e'en

for love, for the strange chance brought him alike grief and joy—joy, from the thought that they were indeed free from guile; sorrow, since he believed what he saw.

And he spake in his heart: "Nay, what may this mean?"

A. L. ROWSE
(1903–1997)

As we scoot round Gribbin Head towards St Austell, let me give you a little warning about this next fella. He can be a bit prickly.

Rowse was a working-class lad, born in Tregonissey, who showed such promise at school that he was championed by Arthur Quiller-Couch. Old Q helped Rowse get into Oxford University, where he became a decorated, if contentious, Elizabethan scholar.

He was a difficult man with an ambivalent relationship to the people and the place of Cornwall but his breadth of interests was, frankly, incredible. He wrote over 100 books, including biographies of Shakespeare and Marlowe, a study of *Homosexuals in History* and *The Cornish in America*, short stories, poetry for children, and the autobiography *A Cornish Childhood*. Much of Rowse's poetry is set in the area we're approaching now around Charlestown (can you see the masts of those tall ships?) and Trenarren, where he lived most of his life.

The Little Land

(*For Marthe Bibesco*)

There is a taste upon the tongue
    if only I could recapture it
Of smouldering summer seas
    running in upon the coast
Or perhaps the sibilance of leaves
    frilled by the breeze from valley's mouth
In the mind such mixture of *wohlgemuth*
    images around the corner of the eye
Of the ferry-boat arriving at the quay
    nosing her way into Percuil
Riverside St Mawes festive and gay
    with tousled summer visitors
Or visiting our toy cathedral town
    from the petunias of Treseder's in Cathedral Lane
    to Pellymounter's musty bookshop in Pydar Street.
How to savour the hours upon the palate
    the honeyed hours of the little land
    with their accumulated memories?
Here is the white gate to Trewithen
    so often passed by with my friend
Now open to me, the hidden pleasances,
    the shadowy park and all within
Panelled rooms of old Sir Christopher
    portraits of Hawkins and Zachary Mudge

a kingdom of camellias beyond.
The garnered riches of my later life
 are everywhere I turn on every hand.
Here beneath the balcony of the Fowey Hotel
 Q. walks once more in the seaward garden
A more distant memory still
 I see myself a schoolboy
Panting up Polruan hill in the hot afternoon
 to Lanteglos Polperro Looe
One Sunday trudging down the lane to Lansallos
 the tower dark against the sunset sky
The bells suddenly burst out ringing
 sweet and clear to evensong
Or looking down from the cliff upon
 the cornered cove at Talland
Blue sea lapsing idly in
 over seaweed and white sand
Presided over by the campanile built
 upon the living rock looking out to sea
Or high on his inland perch
 the hermit of Roche
Beckons from his roofless beacon
 over the moor to Hensbarrow
North Goonbarrow, Lower Ninestones,
 the corrugated ridge of Helman Tor
Dark in the distance lies
 enchanted Luxulyan
Of long boyhood walks up the Valley
 and round by the church
Where ivied traceries on cool

moorstone-mullioned windows
 slaked the thirst of summer and youth
Raging in the mind matted
 with wild convolvulus
Red Admirals feeding on pink
 clumps of hempagrimony
Early lemon shoots of bracken
 and tang of camomile
Filling every crevice of the heart
 with remembered honey stored
To feed on with thanksgiving
 in dark days to come.

JACK CLEMO
(1916–1994)

Maybe there's something about St Austell, but up at Trethosa, a few miles further inland from Rowse's birthplace, we find another awkward character: the poet Jack Clemo.

Clemo's Cornwall is not a comfortable place, and Clemo is not a comfortable poet. He was born into extreme poverty in the china-clay mining region and his father, a clayworker, died when Jack was a baby. The only inheritance his father could leave him was the syphilis he had contracted while working in the copper mines of Montana. Congenital syphilis would lead to Clemo spending the majority of his life deaf and blind and with numerous other physical weaknesses and troubles.

Clemo found symbols for his ravaged body and uncompromising faith in the clay-mining landscape around him, where farms and moorland were being churned up and destroyed – or purified, as Clemo imagined. This violent process became a grand metaphor in his early work, of which 'The Excavator' is a powerful example.

The Excavator

I stand here musing in the rain
This Sabbath evening where the pit-head stain
Of bushes is uprooted, strewn
In waggon-tracks and puddles,
While the fleering downpour fuddles
The few raw flowers along the mouldering dump –
Ridge hollowed and rough-hewn
By the daily grind and thump
Of this grim excavator. It shields me
From lateral rain-gusts, its square body turned
To storm-lashed precipices it has churned.

I feel exultantly
The drip of clayey water from the poised
Still bar above me; thrilling with the rite
Of baptism all my own,
Acknowledging the might
Of God's great arm alone;
Needing no ritual voiced
In speech or earthly idiom to draw
My soul to His new law.

The bars now hinged o'erhead and drooping form
A Cross that lacks the symmetry
Of those in churches, but is more

Like His Whose stooping tore
The vitals from our world's foul secrecy.
This too has power to worm
The entrails from a flint, bearing the scoop
With every searching swoop:
That broken-mouthed gargoyle
Whose iron jaws bite the soil,
Snapping with sadist kisses in the soft
White breasts of rocks, and ripping the sleek belly
Of sprawling clay-mounds, lifting as pounded jelly
Flower-roots and bush-tufts with the reeking sand.
I fondle and understand
In lonely worship this malicious tool.

Yes, this is Christian art
To me men could not school
With delicate aesthetes. Their symbols oft
Tempt simple souls like me
Whom Nature meant to seal
With doom of poetry,
And dowered with eye and brain
Sensitive to the stain
Of Beauty and the grace of man's Ideal.
But I have pressed my way
Past all their barren play
Of intellect, adulthood, the refined
Progressive sickness of the mind
Which throws up hues and shapes alien to God's
Way with a man in a stripped clay desert. Now
I am a child again,

With a child's derision of the mentors' rods
And a child's quick pain,
Loving to stand as now in outlawed glee
Amid the squelching mud and make a vow
With joy no priest or poet takes from me.

I cannot speak their language; I am one
Who feels the doggerel of Heaven
Purge earth of poetry; God's foolishness
Laugh through the web man's ripening wisdom spun;
The world's whole culture riven
By moody excavations Love shall bless.
All staining rhythms of Art and Nature break
Within my mind, turn grey, grow truth
Rigid and ominous as this engine's tooth.
And so I am awake:
No more a man who sees
Colour in flowers or hears from birds a song,
Or dares to worship where the throng
Seek Beauty and its old idolatries.
No altar soils my vision with a lax
Adult appeal to sense,
Or festering harmonies' magniloquence.
My faith and symbol shall be stark.
My hand upon these caterpillar-tracks
Bogged in the mud and clay,
I find it easier to pray:
"Keep far from me all loveliness, O God,
And let me laud
Thy meaner moods, so long unprized;

The motions of that twisted, dark,
Deliberate crucial Will
I feel deep-grinding still
Under the dripping clay with which I am baptized."

SABINE BARING-GOULD
(1834–1924)

I don't know about you, but after Clemo's poem I'm about ready for a song. Now, while the Reverend Sabine Baring-Gould might have lived on the wrong side of the Devon–Cornwall border, he had a song for every occasion and his writing traversed the border. Books such as *Mrs Curgenven of Curgenven*, *In the Roar of the Sea*, *The Gaverocks*, and *In a Quiet Village* were set in a united Devon and Cornwall, which Baring-Gould referred to as the 'West of England' or 'Damnonia' in his books. And his books are legion. Over the years he published novels, stories, hagiographies, biographies and books for children. He wrote studies of werewolves, travel books, books on folklore, books about caves, books of Icelandic sagas, and much, much more. He also collected folk songs, gathered 'from the Mouths of the People', like these.

Lullabye

1

Sleep baby sleep!
   Dad is not nigh,
Tossed on the deep,
   Lul–lul–a–by!
Moon shining bright,
   Dropping of dew.
Owls hoot all night
   To–whit! to–whoo!

2

Sleep, baby, sleep!
   Dad is away,
Tossed on the deep,
   Looking for day.
In the hedge row
   Glow–worms alight,
Rivulets flow,
   All through the night.

3

Sleep baby sleep!
  Dad is afar,
Tossed on the deep,
  Watching a star.
Clock going–tick,
  Tack,–in the dark.
On the hearth – click! –
  Dies the last spark.

4

Sleep, baby, sleep!
  What! not a wink!
Dad on the deep,
  What will he think?
Baby dear, soon
  Daddy will come,
Bringing red shoon
  For baby at home.

Come My Lads

I

Come my lads let us be jolly!
Drive away dull melancholy
For to grieve it is a folly,
  When we're met together.
Come, let's live and well agree,
Always shun bad company,
Why should we not merry merry be,
  When we're met together?
Chorus – Come my lads let us be jolly *&c.*

2

Here's the bottle, as it passes,
Do not fail to fill your glasses,
Water-drinkers are dull asses,
  When they're met together.
Milk is meet for infancy,
Ladies like to sip Bohea,
Not such stuff for you and me
  When we're met together.
Chorus – Come my lads, let us be jolly, *&c.*

Solomon a wise man hoary
Told us quite another story.
In our drink we'll chirp and glory,
          When we're met together.
Come my lads let's sing in chorus,
Merrily, but yet decorous,
Praising all good drinks before us,
          When we're met together.
Chorus – Come my lads, let us be jolly *&c.*

Two Wrestling Songs

When Robert Southey finally did visit Cornwall in 1836, bad weather led to him spending a night at the Red Lion in St Columb Major, where the landlord was one James Polkinghorne, Cornwall's champion wrestler. The first of the following ballads is an account of Polkinghorne's famous bout against the Devonshire champion Abraham Cann. It was written as a broadside ballad, which was essentially a form of early journalism, translating the most sensational news into printed songs to be distributed as cheaply as possible.

The second ballad is a more sombre tale collected by Sabine Baring-Gould. The singer told him that it used to be sung at wrestling events in the town of Liskeard, but we might as well sing them both and as we pass near to Polkinghorne's on our journey west.

The Ballad of Cann and Polkinghorne

When Polkinghorne did first agree,
   And Cann the day did fix, Sir,
It was October twenty-three,
   In eighteen twenty-six, Sir;
And 'twas beside the Tamar stream
   This Wrestling was appointed,
You'd think the crowds they hither came
   To see the Lord's anointed.

The seats were fastened well with clamps,
   For gentlefolks to look on
Cornubia's son in stocking vamps,
   And Cann, who had a shoe on;
And here were brothers, sons, and dad,
   Besides their num'rous friends, Sir,
With ev'ry man could mount a pad,
   From Dorset to Land's End, Sir.

The men shook hands, Cann seized upon
   His opponent's left shoulder,
And he as quickly fasten'd on
   The elbow of the holder;
They both got hitch'd, when, oh, good lack!
   Why who could have portended,

That in five minutes on his back
    Cann thus should lay extended?

One Devon Tryer shook his head
    With wisdom so profound, Sir,
He thought full sure that Cann was dead,
    As he lay on the ground, Sir.
The Devon men sung out—"foul play,"
    And made a hideous clatter,
While some roar'd out—"Why Aby, pray!
    "Why, Aby! what's the matter?"

Cann is a man of as good game,
    As ever yet was born, Sir,
But has not weight nor strength to tame
    The game of Polkinghorne, Sir;
These Cornishmen are such a breed,
    I've freely made my mind up,
To set them down as Adam's seed,
    Instructed by old Jacob.

But Cann rose up with half his crown,
    His bones and feelings sore, Sir,
For Devon ne'er had seen him down
    For nine long years before, Sir;
So after fifteen minutes pause,
    They hitched again and try'd, Sir,
How soon they could decide the cause—
    Who'd be old England's pride, Sir.

Cann, like a donkey, kick'd away,
 To spoil his *understanders*,
But Polky's friends disliked such play,
 And they're not geese nor ganders;
They said it might the dandies shock,
 And give the doctors joy, Sir,
But he must come the Cornish lock,
 Ere he could throw their boy, Sir.

Polk caught Cann round the waist, to try
 The heave was his intent, Sir,
But he was ready instantly,
 His aim for to prevent, Sir,
Cann lock'd his foot right firm and fast,
 Both acted very clever,
Polk could not heave—the time was past,
 And both fell down together.

The Tryers, then, on either side,
 They had a full hour's contest,
But as they could not it decide,
 To toss they thought it was best;
'Twas Cann's hard fate to meet the loss,
 Though sure as he was born, Sir,
He had a better chance at toss
 Than tossing Polkinghorne, Sir.

Then, coming to the scratch again,
 Each man was very hearty,
They us'd their utmost pow'rs amain,

In hopes to please their party:
When Cann was thrown—what Devon felt
   I need not here repeat, Sir,
But Polkinghorne got the belt,
   And then rode off in state, Sir.

A dreadful clamour then arose,
   Devonia said—"No fall," Sir,
'Twas thought indeed they'd come to blows,
   To make it but a *foil*, Sir.
So Polkinghorne was borne amain,
   By all his friends desire, Sir,
But Devon wish'd him back again,
   In hopes that he might tire, Sir.

The *Alfred* Journal did report
   That it was *not a fall*, Sir,
And, judging it by Devon sport,
   It only was a *foil*, Sir;
But if his paper it had got,
   In number such a *fall*, Sir,
He'd think how hard had been his lot
   To meet with such a *foil*, Sir.

Now Cann himself, as I've been told,
   Says he was thrown for certain,
But Devon bets would want such gold—
   My eye and Betty Martin!
With heavy hearts and pockets light,
   The Devon men departed,

The Cornishmen they were all right,
   And for St. Columb started.

I fear my song is much too long,
   So pardon I must crave, Sir,
And as my voice it is not strong,
   This shall be the last stave, Sir,
So while the hero's health you put,
   To Devon I must say, Sir,
Though Cann can shuffle and can cut,
   With Polk he cannot play, Sir.

The Wrestling Match

I sing of champions bold,
That wrestled not for gold.
    And all the cry was Will Trefry!
That he should win the day.
So, Will Trefry Huzzah!
The ladies clap their hands and cry
    Trefry! Trefry! Huzzah!

2

Then up sprang little Jan,
A lad scarce grown a man,
    He said, Trefry! I wot, I'll try
A hitch with thee this day.
So, little Jan, Huzzah!
The ladies clap their hands and cry,
    O little Jan, Huzzah!

3

They wrestled on the ground
His match Trefry had found
    And back he bore, in struggle sore,
He felt his force give way.

So little Jan, Huzzah!
So some did say—but others, Nay,
 Trefry! Trefry! Huzzah!

4

Then with a desperate toss,
Will showed the flying hoss.
 And little Jan fell on the tan,
And never more he spake.
O little Jan! alack!
The ladies say, O woe's the day,
 O little Jan – alack!

5

Now little Jan, I ween,
That day had married been;
 Had he not died, a gentle bride,
That day he home had led.
The ladies sigh, the ladies cry
 O little Jan is dead!

ARTHUR CONAN DOYLE
(1859–1930)

Yes, London's great detective came to Cornwall – and to Poldhu! This Sherlock Holmes story appeared in 1910, almost immediately after Sir Arthur Conan Doyle's own Cornish adventure. Both were here, ostensibly, for convalescence, but neither appears to have relaxed exactly. Conan Doyle quickly wrote a new Holmes story (published the very same year), while Holmes found himself at the centre of a mystery. 'The Adventure of the Devil's Foot' was one of Conan Doyle's favourite Holmes stories.

We pick up with Holmes and Watson at the beginning of their quiet coastal recuperation, settling into the holiday cottage and taking in the scenery. Naturally, their peace would not last long.

from 'The Adventure of the Devil's Foot'

Thus it was that in the early spring of that year we found ourselves together in a small cottage near Poldhu Bay, at the further extremity of the Cornish peninsula.

It was a singular spot, and one peculiarly well suited to the grim humour of my patient. From the windows of our little white-washed house, which stood high upon a grassy headland, we looked down upon the whole sinister semi-circle of Mounts Bay, that old death trap of sailing vessels, with its fringe of black cliffs and surge-swept reefs on which innumerable seamen have met their end. With a northerly breeze it lies placid and sheltered, inviting the storm-tossed craft to tack into it for rest and protection.

Then comes the sudden swirl round of the wind, the blustering gale from the south-west, the dragging anchor, the lee shore, and the last battle in the creaming breakers. The wise mariner stands far out from that evil place.

On the land side our surroundings were as sombre as on the sea. It was a country of rolling moors, lonely and dun-coloured, with an occasional church tower to mark the site of some old-world village. In every direction upon these moors there were traces of some vanished race which had passed utterly away, and left as its sole record strange monuments of stone, irregular mounds which contained the burned ashes of the dead, and curious earthworks which hinted at prehistoric strife. The glamour and mystery of the place, with its sinister atmosphere of forgotten nations, appealed to the imagination of my friend, and he spent much of his time in long walks and solitary meditations upon the moor. The ancient Cornish language had also arrested his attention, and he had, I remember, conceived the idea that it was akin to the Chaldean, and had been largely derived from the Phœnician traders in tin. He had received a consignment of books upon philology and was settling down to develop this thesis, when suddenly, to my sorrow and to his unfeigned delight, we found ourselves, even in that land of dreams, plunged into a problem at our very doors which was more intense, more engrossing, and infinitely more mysterious than any of those which had driven us from London. Our simple life and peaceful, healthy routine were violently interrupted, and we were precipitated into the midst of a series of events which caused the utmost excitement not only in Cornwall, but throughout the whole West of England. Many of my readers may retain some recollection of what was called at the time "The Cornish Horror," though a most imperfect account of the matter reached the London Press. Now, after thirteen years, I will give the true details of this inconceivable affair to the public.

I have said that scattered towers marked the villages which dotted this part of Cornwall. The nearest of these was the hamlet of Tredannick Wollas, where the cottages of a couple of hundred inhabitants clustered round an ancient, moss-grown church. The vicar of the parish, Mr. Roundhay, was something of an archæologist, and as such Holmes had made his acquaintance. He was a middle-aged man, portly and affable, with a considerable fund of local lore. At his invitation we had taken tea at the vicarage, and had come to know, also, Mr. Mortimer Tregennis, an independent gentleman, who increased the clergyman's scanty resources by taking rooms in his large, straggling house. The vicar, being a bachelor, was glad to come to such an arrangement, though he had little in common with his lodger, who was a thin, dark, spectacled man, with a stoop which gave the impression of actual, physical deformity. I remember that during our short visit we found the vicar garrulous, but his lodger strangely reticent, a sad-faced, introspective man, sitting with averted eyes, brooding apparently upon his own affairs.

These were the two men who entered abruptly into our little sitting-room on Tuesday, March the 16th, shortly after our breakfast hour, as we were smoking together, preparatory to our daily excursion upon the moors.

"Mr. Holmes," said the vicar, in an agitated voice, "the most extraordinary and tragic affair has occurred during the night. It is the most unheard-of business. We can only regard it as a special Providence that you should chance to be here at the time, for in all England you are the one man we need."

I glared at the intrusive vicar with no very friendly eyes; but Holmes toke his pipe from his lips and sat up in his chair like an old hound who hears the view-halloa. He waved his hand to the sofa, and our palpitating visitor with his agitated companion sat side by side upon it. Mr. Mortimer Tregennis was more self-contained than the clergyman, but the twitching of his thin hands and the brightness of his dark eyes showed that they shared a common emotion.

"Shall I speak or you?" he asked of the vicar.

"Well, as you seem to have made the discovery, what-ever it may be, and the vicar to have had it second-hand, perhaps you had better do the speaking," said Holmes.

I glanced at the hastily-clad clergyman, with the formally-dressed lodger seated beside him, and was amused at the surprise which Holmes's simple deduc-tion had brought to their faces.

"Perhaps I had best say a few words first," said the vicar, "and then you can judge if you will listen to the details from Mr. Tregennis, or whether we should not hasten at once to the scene of this mysterious affair. I may explain, then, that our friend here spent last even-ing in the company of his two brothers, Owen and George, and of his sister Brenda, at their house of Tre-dannick Wartha, which is near the old stone cross upon the moor. He left them shortly after ten o'clock, playing cards round the dining-room table, in excellent health and spirits. This morning, being an early riser, he walked in that direction before breakfast, and was over-taken by the carriage of Dr. Richards, who explained that he had just been sent for on a most urgent call to Tredannick Wartha. Mr. Mortimer Tregennis naturally went with him. When he arrived at Tredannick Wartha he found an extraordinary state of things. His two brothers and his sister were seated round the table exactly as he had left them, the cards still spread in front of them and the candles burned down to their sockets. The sister lay back stone-dead in her chair, while the two brothers sat on each side of her laughing, shouting, and singing, the senses stricken clean out of them. All three of them, the dead woman and the two demented men, retained upon their faces an expression of the utmost horror—a convulsion of terror which was dreadful to look upon. There was no sign of the presence of anyone in the house, except Mrs. Porter, the old cook and housekeeper, who declared that she had slept deeply and heard no sound during the night. Nothing had been stolen or disarranged, and there is absolutely no explanation of what the horror can be which has frightened a woman to death and two strong men out of their senses. There is the situation, Mr. Holmes, in a nutshell, and if you can help us to clear it up you will have done a great work."

I had hoped that in some way I could coax my companion back into the quiet which had been the object of our journey; but one glance at his intense face and contracted eyebrows told me how vain was now the expectation. He sat for some little time in silence, absorbed in the strange drama which had broken in upon our peace.

"I will look into this matter," he said at last. "On the face of it, it would appear to be a case of a very exceptional nature. Have you been there yourself, Mr. Roundhay?"

"No, Mr. Holmes. Mr. Tregennis brought back the account to the vicarage, and I at once hurried over with him to consult you."

"How far is it to the house where this singular tragedy occurred?"

"About a mile inland."

"Then we shall walk over together. But, before we start, I must ask you a few questions, Mr. Mortimer Tregennis."

The other had been silent all this time, but I had observed that his more controlled excitement was even greater than the obtrusive emotion of the clergyman. He sat with a pale, drawn face, his anxious gaze fixed upon Holmes, and his thin hands clasped convulsively together. His pale lips quivered as he listened to the dreadful experience which had befallen his family, and his dark eyes seemed to reflect something of the horror of the scene.

"Ask what you like, Mr. Holmes," said he eagerly. "It is a bad thing to speak of, but I will answer you the truth."

"Tell me about last night."

"Well, Mr. Holmes, I supped there, as the vicar has said, and my elder brother George proposed a game of whist afterwards. We sat down about nine o'clock. It was a quarter-past ten when I moved to go. I left them all round the table, as merry as could be."

"Who let you out?"

"Mrs. Porter had gone to bed, so I let myself out. I shut the hall door behind me. The window of the room in which they sat was closed, but the blind was not drawn down. There was no change in door or window this morning, nor any reason to think that any stranger had been to the house. Yet there they sat, driven clean mad with terror, and Brenda lying dead of fright, with her head hanging over the arm of the chair. I'll never get the sight of that room out of my mind so long as I live."

"The facts, as you state them, are certainly most remarkable," said Holmes. "I take it that you have no theory yourself which can in any way account for them?"

"It's devilish, Mr. Holmes; devilish!" cried Mortimer Tregennis. "It is not of this world. Something has come into that room which has dashed the light of reason from their minds. What human contrivance could do that?"

"I fear," said Holmes, "that if the matter is beyond humanity it is certainly beyond me. Yet we must exhaust all natural explanations before we fall back upon such a theory as this. As to yourself, Mr. Tregennis, I take it you were divided in some way from your family, since they lived together and you had rooms apart?"

"That is so, Mr. Holmes, though the matter is past and done with. We were a family of tin-miners at Redruth, but we sold out our venture to a company, and so retired with enough to keep us. I won't deny that there was some feeling about the division of the money and it stood between us for a time, but it was all forgiven and forgotten, and we were the best of friends together."

"Looking back at the evening which you spent together, does anything stand out in your memory as throwing any possible light upon the tragedy? Think carefully, Mr. Tregennis, for any clue which can help me."

"There is nothing at all, sir."

"Your people were in their usual spirits?"

"Never better."

"Were they nervous people? Did they ever show any apprehension of coming danger?"

"Nothing of the kind."

"You have nothing to add then, which could assist me?"

Mortimer Tregennis considered earnestly for a moment.

"There is one thing occurs to me," said he at last. "As we sat at the table my back was to the window, and my brother George, he being my partner at cards, was facing it. I saw him once look hard over my shoulder, so I turned round and looked also. The blind was up and the window shut, but I could just make out the bushes on the lawn, and it seemed to me for a moment that I saw something moving among them. I couldn't even say if it were man or animal, but I just thought there was something there. When I asked him what he was looking at, he told me that he had the same feeling. That is all that I can say."

"Did you not investigate?"

"No; the matter passed as unimportant."

"You left them, then, without any premonition of evil?"

"None at all."

"I am not clear how you came to hear the news so early this morning."

"I am an early riser, and generally take a walk before breakfast. This morning I had hardly started when the doctor in his carriage overtook me. He told me that old Mrs. Porter had sent a boy down with an urgent message. I sprang in beside him and we drove on. When we got there we looked into that dreadful room. The candles and the fire must have burned out hours before, and they had been sitting there in the dark until dawn had broken. The doctor said Brenda must have been dead at least six hours. There were no signs of violence. She just lay across the arm of the chair with that look on her face. George and Owen were singing snatches of songs and gibbering like two great apes. Oh, it was awful to see! I couldn't stand it, and the doctor was as white as a sheet. Indeed, he fell into a chair in a sort of faint, and we nearly had him on our hands as well."

"Remarkable—most remarkable!" said Holmes, rising and taking his hat. "I think, perhaps, we had better go down to Tredannick Wartha without further delay. I confess that I have seldom known a case which at first sight presented a more singular problem."

DINAH CRAIK
(1826–1887)

We've got a spot of weather coming in, so we'll hole up at the Lizard a minute with Dinah Craik. Craik was a popular novelist in her day and she visited Cornwall in 1881 to write this characterful travel book.

Throughout the journey, Craik, enamoured with the stories of King Arthur and his knights, would compare the folk she met with characters from Malory's *Morte D'Arthur*, which she had brought with her to read. 'One cannot imagine Sir Tristram or Sir Launcelot occupied in spearing a small sand-eel', she writes disapprovingly, while one of her guides, John Curgenven, frequently reminds her of 'some old knight of the Round Table', or even King Arthur himself.

Craik is in turn pompous, kind and patronizing, while always affable and interested in the people she meets. Oop! Here comes the rain.

from An Unsentimental
Journey Through Cornwall

"Hope for the best, and be prepared for the worst," had been the motto of our journey. So when we rose to one of the wettest mornings that ever came out of the sky, there was a certain satisfaction in being prepared for it.

"We must have a fire, that is certain," was our first decision. This entailed the abolition of our beautiful decorations—our sea-holly and ferns; also some anxious looks from our handmaiden. Apparently no fire had been lit in this rather despised room for many months—years perhaps—and the chimney rather resented being used. A few agonised down-puffs greatly interfered with the comfort of the breakfast table, and an insane attempt to open the windows made matters worse.

Which was most preferable—to be stifled or deluged? We were just considering the question, when the chimney took a new and kinder thought, or the wind took a turn—it seemed to blow alternately from every quarter, and then from all quarters at once—the smoke went up straight, the room grew warm and bright, with the cosy peace of the first fire of the season. Existence became once more endurable, nay, pleasant.

"We shall survive, spite of the rain!" And we began to laugh over our lost day which we had meant to begin by bathing in Housel Cove; truly, just to stand outside the door would give an admirable douche bath in three minutes. "But how nice it is to be inside, with a roof over our heads, and no necessity for travelling. Fancy the unfortunate tourists who have fixed on to-day for visiting the Lizard!" (Charles had told us that Monday was a favourite day for excursions.) "Fancy anybody being obliged to go out such weather as this!"

And in our deep pity for our fellow-creatures we forgot to pity ourselves.

Nor was there much pity needed; we had provided against emergencies, with a good store of needlework and knitting, anything that would pack in small compass, also a stock of unquestionably "light" literature—paper-covered, double-columned, sixpenny volumes, inclosing an amount of enjoyment which those only can understand who are true lovers of Walter Scott. We had enough of him to last for a week of wet days. And we had a one-volume Tennyson, all complete, and a "Morte d'Arthur"—Sir Thomas Malory's. On this literary provender we felt that as yet we should not starve.

Also, some little fingers having a trifling turn for art, brought out triumphantly a colour-box, pencils, and pictures. And the wall-paper being one of the very ugliest that ever eye beheld, we sought and obtained permission to adorn it with these, our *chefs-d'œuvre*, pasted at regular intervals. Where we hope they still remain, for the edification of succeeding lodgers.

We read the "Idylls of the King" all through, finishing with "The Passing of Arthur," where the "bold Sir Bedivere" threw Excalibur into the mere—which is supposed to be Dozmare Pool. Here King Arthur's faithful lover was so melted—for the hundredth time—by the pathos of the story, and by many old associations, that the younger and more practical minds grew scornful, and declared that probably King Arthur had never existed at all—or if he had, was nothing but a rough barbarian, unlike even the hero of Sir Thomas Malory, and far more unlike the noble modern gentleman of Tennyson's verse. Maybe: and yet, seeing that

> "Tis better to have loved and lost
> Than never to have loved at all,"

may it not be better to have believed in an impossible ideal man, than to accept contentedly a low ideal, and worship blindly the worldly, the mean, or the base?

This topic furnished matter for so much hot argument, that, besides doing a quantity of needlework, we succeeded in making our one wet day by no means the least amusing of our seventeen days in Cornwall.

Hour after hour we watched the rain—an even downpour. In the midst of it we heard a rumour that Charles had been seen about the town, and soon after he appeared at the door, hat in hand, soaked but smiling, to inquire for and sympathise with his ladies. Yes, he *had* brought a party to the Lizard that day!—unfortunate souls (or bodies), for there could not have been a dry thread left on them! We gathered closer round our cosy fire; ate our simple dinner with keen enjoyment, and agreed that after all we had much to be thankful for.

In the afternoon the storm abated a little, and we

thought we would seize the chance of doing some shopping, if there was a shop in Lizard Town. So we walked—I ought rather to say waded, for the road was literally swimming—meeting not one living creature, except a family of young ducks, who, I need scarcely say, were enjoying supreme felicity.

"Yes, ladies, this is the sort of weather we have pretty well all winter. Very little frost or snow, but rain and storm, and plenty of it. Also fogs; I've heard there's nothing anywhere like the fogs at the Lizard."

So said the woman at the post-office, which, except the serpentine shops, seemed to be the one emporium of commerce in the place. There we could get all we wanted, and a good deal that we were very thankful we did not want, of eatables, drinkables, and wearables. Also ornaments, china vases, &c., of a kind that would have driven frantic any person of æsthetic tastes. Among them an active young Cornishman of about a year old was meandering aimlessly, or with aims equally destructive to himself and the community. He all but succeeded in bringing down a row of plates upon his devoted head, and then tied himself up, one fat finger after another, in a ball of twine, upon which he began to howl violently.

"He's a regular little trial," said the young mother proudly. "He's only sixteen months old, and yet he's up to all sorts of mischief. I don't know what in the world I shall do with he, presently. Naughty boy!" with a delighted scowl.

"Not naughty, only active," suggested another maternal spirit, and pleaded that the young jackanapes should be found something to do that was not mischief, but yet would occupy his energies, and fill his mind. At which, the bright bold face looked up as if he had understood it all—an absolutely fearless face, brimming with fun, and shrewdness too. Who knows? The "regular little trial' may grow into a valuable member of society—fisherman, sailor, coastguardman—daring and doing heroic deeds; perhaps saving many a life on nights such as last night, which had taught us what Cornish coast-life was all winter through.

The storm was now gradually abating; the wind had lulled entirely, the rain had ceased, and by sunset a broad yellow streak all along the west implied that it might possibly be a fine day to-morrow.

But the lane was almost a river still, and the slippery altitudes of the "hedges" were anything but desirable. As the only possible place for a walk I ventured into a field where two or three cows cropped their supper of damp grass round one of those green hillocks seen in every Cornish pasture field—a manure heap planted with cabbages, which grow there with a luxuriance that turns ugliness into positive beauty. Very dreary everything was—the soaking grass, the leaden sky, the angry-looking sea, over which a rainy moon was just beginning to throw a faint glimmer; while shorewards one could just trace the outline of Lizard Point and the wheat-field behind it. Yesterday those fields had looked so sunshiny and fair, but to-night they were all dull and grey, with rows of black dots indicating the soppy, sodden harvest sheaves.

Which reminded me that to-morrow was the harvest festival at Landewednack, when all the world and his wife was invited by shilling tickets to have tea in the rectory garden, and afterwards to assist at the evening thanksgiving service in the church.

"Thanksgiving! What for?" some poor farmer might well exclaim, especially on such a day as this. Some harvest festivals must occasionally seem a bitter mockery. Indeed, I doubt if the next generation will not be wise in taking our "Prayers for Rain," "Prayers for Fair Weather," clean out of the liturgy. Such conceited intermeddling with the government of the world sounds to some ridiculous, to others actually profane. "Snow and hail, mists and vapours, wind and storm, fulfilling His Word." And it must be fulfilled, no matter at what cost to individuals or to nations. The laws of the universe must be carried out, even though the mystery of sorrow, like the still greater mystery of evil, remains for ever unexplained. "Shall not the Judge of all the earth do right?"

And how right is His right! How marvellously beautiful He can make this world! until we can hardly imagine anything more beautiful in the world everlasting. Ay, even after such a day as to-day, when the world seems hardly worth living in, yet we live on, live to wake up unto such a to-morrow—

But I must wait to speak of it in another page.

HAL-AN-TOW
collected by Sabine Baring-Gould

Helston's Flora Day is an annual celebration that occurs on 8 May, marked by dance and song. It is not 'till late at night', as Baring-Gould says, 'that the town returns to its peaceful propriety.' It is Baring-Gould's version of the 'Hal-an-tow' we have here. He collected and 'corrected' the song and described the celebrations thus:

> Very early in the morning, a party of youths and maidens goes into the country, and returns dancing through the streets to a quaint tune, peculiar to the day, called the 'Furry Dance'. At eight o'clock the 'Hal-an-tow' is sung by a party of from twenty to thirty men and boys who come into the town bearing green branches, with flowers in their hats, preceded by a single drum, on which a boy beats the Furry Dance. They perambulate the town for many hours, stopping at intervals at some of the principal houses.

Hal-an-tow

1

Robin Hood and little John
  They both are gone to the fair, O!
And we will go to the merry green wood,
  To see what they do there, O!
      And for to chase, O, to chase the buck
        and doe!
     With Hal-an-tow, jolly rumble, O,
    And we were up as soon as the day, O,
     For to fetch the Summer home,
   The Summer, and the May, O!
    Now the Winter is a gone, O.

2

Where are those Spaniards,
  That make so great a boast, O!
Why, they shall eat the grey goose feathers,
  And we will eat the roast, O!
      In every land, O, the land where'er we go,
      With Hal-an-tow, jolly rumble O
Chorus. And we were up, *&c*:

3

As for that good Knight, S. George,
  S. George he was a Knight, O
Of all the knights in Christendom!
  S. George he is the right, O!
        In every land, O! the land where'er we go,
        With Hal-an-tow, jolly rumble O
Chorus. And we were up, *&c:*

4

God bless Modryb Maria
  And all her power and might, O!
And send us peace in merry England.
  Send peace by day and night, O!
        To merry England, O! both now and
        ever mo'
        With Hal-an-tow, jolly rumble O
Chorus. And we were up, *&c.*

HUMPHRY DAVY
(1778–1829)

We should have a laugh here. Or we will if Sir Humphry's got the gas running. See, Humphry Davy is the Penzance-born chemist known today for his work on nitrous oxide – laughing gas – and for inventing the Davy Lamp, which saved the lives of innumerable miners.

Important as this was to us, still it barely scratches the surface of Davy's influence. In his day, Davy was among the most celebrated men in Europe. As a young man he upped sticks to Bristol, falling in with Samuel Taylor Coleridge and Robert Southey. Coleridge would remain a close friend until Davy's death. Davy would even edit the proofs of the updated *Lyrical Ballads*, sent to him by another friend, William Wordsworth. As his fame grew, so too did his social circle, extending to Walter Scott and Lord Byron (Davy is passingly mentioned in 'Don Juan'), and even Johann Wolfgang von Goethe, with whom Davy would stay in Germany.

Poetry was not Davy's chief gift to the world. It's his chemical and medical work and his work at the Royal Institution (Davy was the institution's first director) that secure him his place in history.

The following 'Lines' were published in Robert Southey's *The Annual Anthology* in 1800.

Lines

Descriptive of feelings produced by a Visit to the place
where the first nineteen years of my Life were spent, in
a stormy day, after an absence of thirteen months.

Thou Ocean dark and terrible in storms!
My eye is closed upon thee, and I view
The light of other days. The sunbeams dance
Upon thy waves, the purple clouds of morn
Hang o'er thy rocks resplendent. Scenes beloved!
Scenes of my youth! within my throbbing breast
Ye have awakened rapture. Round me crowd
Tumultuous passions, all the joys and cares
Of Infancy, the glittering dreams of youth
Ambitious and energic.
                              Here my eyes
First trembled with the lustre of the day,
And here the gently-soothing sounds of love
First lulled my feeble spirit to repose.
Here first a mother's care awoke my sense
To mild enjoyment. Here my opening mind
First in the mingled harmony of voice
And speaking countenance, astonished read
Another's living feelings and his thoughts.
Here first I woo'd thee Nature, in the forms
Of majesty and freedom, and thy charms
Soft mingling with the sports of infancy
Its rising social passions and its wants

Intense and craving, kindled into one
Supreme emotion.

                Hence awoke to life
Sublimest thoughts, a living energy
That still has warm'd my beating heart, and still
Its objects varying, has impelled me on
To various action.

                Here the novel sense
Of beauty thrilling through my new-tuned frame,
Called into being gentlest sympathies:
Then through the trembling moonshine of the grove
My earliest lays were wafted by the breeze.
Here first my serious spirit learnt to trace
The mystic laws, from whose high energy
The moving atoms in eternal change
Still rise to animation.

                Many days
Are passed, O scene beloved! since last my eyes
Beheld the moon-beams gild thy foaming waves.
Ambitious then, confiding in her powers,
Spurning her prison, onward flew my soul
To mingle with her kindred. In the breeze
That wafts futurity upon its wings
To hear the sounds of praise.

                And not in vain
Have those high hopes existed. Not in vain
The dew of labor has oppressed my brow,
On which the rose of pleasure never glow'd;
For I have tasted of that sacred stream
Of Science, whose delicious waters flow

From Nature's bosom. I have felt the warm,
The gentle influence of congenial souls
Whose kindred hopes have cheered me. Who have
    taught
My irritable spirit how to bear
Injustice and oppression, nor to droop
In its high flight beneath the feeble rage
Of noisy tempests, whose kind hands have given
New plumes of rapture to my drooping wing
When ruffled by their wild and angry breath.
Beloved rocks! thou Ocean, white with mist
Once more ye live upon my humid eyes,
Again ye waken in my throbbing breast
The sympathies of Nature.
                              Now I go
Once more to visit my remembered home,
With heart-felt rapture, there to mingle tears
Of purest joy, to feel the extatic glow
Of warm affection, and again to view
The rosy light that shone upon my youth.

R. M. BALLANTYNE
(1825–1894)

The mine shafts of Botallack stretch far under the sea and some of the more dramatic engine houses can still be seen today perched on the cliffs above St Just in Penwith. Ballantyne made several trips into their tunnels and shafts to familiarize himself with the conditions and the people who spent their lives in this underworld. It impressed him profoundly and became the setting of his novel *Deep Down*; a page-turner full of smugglers, swindlers and miners.

Ballantyne's enthusiasm for his research reveals itself not only in the dramatic and evocative chapters underground but also in the meandering detours he takes to tell the legends of fairies and giants, or anachronistic royal visits, or to consider the travels of Wesley and the Methodists.

Here, we follow the young doctor Oliver Trembath, who has returned to Cornwall to visit his uncle at St Just. But the way to St Just is more adventuresome than the doctor expected, the danger beginning when he pauses for a swim.

from Deep Down

Misjudging, in his ignorance, the tremendous power of the surf into which he sprang, and daring to recklessness in the conscious possession of unusual strength and courage, he did not pause to look or consider, but at once struck out to sea. He was soon beyond the influence of the breaking waves, and for some time sported in the full enjoyment of the briny Atlantic waters. Then turning towards the shore he swam in and was speedily tossing among the breakers. As he neared the sandy beach and felt the full power of the water on his partially exhausted frame, he experienced a slight feeling of anxiety, for the thunder of each wave as it fell, and rushed up before him in seething foam, seemed to indicate a degree of force which he had not realized in his first vigorous plunge into the sea. A moment more and a wave caught him in its curling crest, and swept him onwards. For the first time in his life, Oliver Trembath's massive strength was of no avail to him. He felt like a helpless infant. In another instant the breaker fell and swept him with irresistible violence up the beach amid a turmoil of hissing foam. No sooner did he touch the ground than he sprang to his feet, and staggered forward a few paces, but the returning rush of water swept sand and stones from beneath his feet, carried his legs from under him, and hurled him back into the hollow of the succeeding wave, which again rolled him on the sand.

Although somewhat stunned, Oliver did not lose consciousness or self-possession. He now fully realized the extreme danger of his position, and the thought flashed through his brain that, at the furthest, his fate must be decided in two or three minutes. Acting on a brave spirit, this thought nerved him to desperate effort. The instant he could plant his feet firmly he bounded forwards, and then, before the backward rush of water had gathered strength, fell on his knees, and dug his fingers and toes deep into the sand. Had the grasp been on something firm he could easily have held on, but the treacherous sand crumbled out of his grasp, and a second time he was carried back into the sea.

The next time he was cast on the beach he felt that his strength was failing; he staggered forward as soon as he touched bottom, with all the energy of one who avails himself of his last chance, but the angry water was too strong for him; feeling that he was being overpowered, he cast his arms up in the air, and gave utterance to a loud cry. It was not like a cry of despair, but sounded more like what one might suppose would be the shout of a brave soldier when compelled to give way—fighting—before the might of overwhelming force. At that moment a hand caught the young man's wrist, and held it for a few seconds in a powerful grasp. The wave retreated, a staggering effort followed, and the next moment Oliver stood panting on the beach grasping the rough hand of his deliverer.

"Semen to me you was pretty nigh gone, sur," said

the man, who had come thus opportunely to the rescue, as he wrung the seawater from his garments.

He was a man of middle height, but of extremely powerful frame, and was habited in the garb of a fisherman.

"Truly I had been gone altogether but for your timely assistance; may God reward you for it!" said Oliver earnestly.

"Well, I don't think you would be so ready to thank me if you did knaw I had half made up my mind to lev'ee go."

Oliver looked at the man in some surprise, for he spoke gruffly, almost angrily, and was evidently in earnest.

"You are jesting," said he incredulously.

"Jestin'; no I ain't, maister. Do 'ee see the boat out over?" he said, pointing to a small craft full of men which was being rowed swiftly round a point not more than half a mile distant; "the villains are after me. They might as well have tried to kitch a cunger by the tail as nab Jim Cuttance in one of his dens, if he hadn't bin forced by the softness of his 'art to pull a young fool out o' the say. You'll have to help me to fight, lad, as I've saved your life. Come, follow me to the cave."

"But—my clothes—" said Oliver, glancing round him in search of his garments.

"They're all safe up here; come along, sur, an' look sharp."

At any other time and in other circumstances Oliver Trembath's fiery spirit would have resented the tone and

130

manner of this man's address, but the feeling that he owed his life to him, and that in some way he appeared to be the innocent cause of bringing misfortune on him, induced him to restrain his feelings and obey without question the mandate of his rescuer. Jim Cuttance led the way to a cave in the rugged cliffs, the low entrance to which was concealed by a huge mass of granite. The moment they entered, several voices burst forth in abuse of the fisherman for his folly in exposing himself, but the latter only replied with a sarcastic laugh, and advised his comrades to get ready for action, for he had been seen by the enemy, who would be down on them directly. At the same time he pointed to Oliver's clothes, which lay in a recess in the side of the cavern.

The youth dressed himself rapidly, and, while thus engaged, observed that there were five men in the cavern, besides his guide, with whom they retired into the farthest recess of the place, and entered into an animated and apparently angry, though low-toned, conversation. At length their leader, for such he evidently was, swung away from them, exclaiming with a laugh: "Well, well, he's a good recruit, and if he should peach on we—us can—"

He concluded the sentence with a significant grunt.

"Now, sur," he said, advancing with his comrade towards Oliver, who was completing his toilet, "they'll be here in ten minutes, an' it is expected that you will lend we a hand. Here's a weapon for you."

So saying, he handed a large pistol to Oliver, who received it with some hesitation.

"I trust that your cause is a good one," he said. "You cannot expect me to fight for you, even though I am indebted to you for my life, without knowing against whom I fight, and why."

At this a tall, thick-set man suddenly cocked his pistol, and uttering a fierce oath swore that if the stranger would not fight, he'd shoot him through the head.

"Silence, Joe Tonkin!" cried Jim Cuttance, in a tone that at once subdued the man.

Oliver, whose eyes had flashed like those of a tiger, drew himself up, and said, "Look at me, lads; I have no desire to boast of what I can or will do, but I assure you it would be as easy to turn back the rising tide as to force me to fight against my will—except, indeed, with yourselves. As I have said, I owe my life to your leader, and apparently have been the innocent means of drawing his enemies upon him. Gratitude tells me to help him if I can, and help him I will if the cause be not a bad one."

"Well spoken, sur," said the leader, with an approving nod; "see to the weapons, Maggot, and I'll explain it all to the gentleman."

So saying, he took Oliver aside, told him hurriedly that the men who were expected to attack them were fishermen belonging to a neighbouring cove, whose mackerel nets had been accidentally cut by his boat some weeks ago, and who were bent on revenge, not believing that the thing had been done by accident.

"But surely you don't mean to use fire-arms against them in such a quarrel?" said Oliver.

A sort of humorous smile crossed the swarthy countenance of the man as he replied:

"They will use pistols against we."

"Be that as it may," said Oliver; "I will never consent to risk taking the life of a countryman in such a cause."

"But you can't fight without a weapon," said the man; "and sure, if 'ee don't shut them they'll shut you."

"No matter, I'll take my chance," said Oliver; "my good cudgel would have served me well enough, but it seems to have been swept away by the sea; here, however, is a weapon that will suit me admirably," he added, picking up a heavy piece of driftwood that lay at his feet.

"Well, if you scat their heads with that, they won't want powder and lead," observed the other with a grin, as he rose and returned to the entrance of the cave, where he warned his comrades to keep as quiet as mice.

The boat which had caused so much angry discussion among the men of the cave had by this time neared the beach, and one of the crew stood up in the bow to guide her into the narrow cove, which formed but a slight protection, even in calm weather, against the violence of that surf which never ceases to grind at the hard rocks of West Cornwall. At length they effected a landing, and the crew, consisting of nine men armed with pistols and cutlasses, hurried up to the cliffs and searched for the entrance to the cavern.

While the events which have been related were taking place, the shades of evening had been gradually creeping over land and sea, and the light was at that time scarcely sufficient to permit of things being distinguished clearly beyond a few yards. The men in the cavern hid themselves in the dark recesses on each side of the entrance, ready for the approaching struggle.

Oliver crouched beside his rescuer with the piece of driftwood by his side. Turning suddenly to his companion, he said, in an almost inaudible whisper:

"Friend, it did not occur to me before, but the men we are about to fight with will recognize me again if we should ever chance to meet; could I not manage to disguise myself in some way?"

"If you get shut," replied his companion in the same low tone, "it won't matter much; but see here—shut your eyes."

Without further remark the man took a handful of wet earth and smeared it over Oliver's face, then, clapping his own "sou'-wester" on his head, he said, with a soft chuckle, "There, your own mother wouldn't knaw 'ee!"

Just then footsteps were heard approaching, and the shadow of a man was seen to rest for a moment on the gravel without. The mouth of the cave was so well hidden, however, that he failed to observe it, and passed on, followed by several of his comrades. Suddenly one of them stopped and said:

"Hold on, lads, it can't be far off, I'm sartin sure; I seed 'em disappear hereabouts."

"You're right," cried Jim Cuttance, with a fierce roar, as he rushed from the cavern and fired full at the man who had spoken. The others followed, and a volley of shots succeeded, while shouts of defiance and anger burst forth on all sides. Oliver sprang out at the same moment with the leader, and rushed on one of the boat's crew with such violence, that his foot slipped on a piece of seaweed and precipitated him to the ground at the man's feet; the other, having sprung forward to meet him, was unable to check himself, tripped over his shoulders and fell on the top of him. The man named Maggot having been in full career close behind Oliver, tumbled over both, followed by another man named John Cock. The others observing them down, rushed with a shout to the rescue, just as Oliver, making a superhuman effort, flung the two men off his back and leaped to his feet. Maggot and the boatman also sprang up, and the latter turned and made for the boat at full speed, seeing that his comrades, overcome by the suddenness of the onset, were in retreat, fighting as they went.

All of them succeeded in getting into the boat unharmed, and were in the act of pushing off, when Jim Cuttance, burning with indignation, leaped into the water, grasped the bow of the boat, and was about to plunge his cutlass into the back of the man nearest him, when he was seized by a strong hand from behind and held back. Next moment the boat was beyond his reach.

Turning round fiercely, the man saw that it was Oliver Trembath who had interfered. He uttered a terrible oath and sprang on him like a tiger; Oliver stood firm, parried with the piece of driftwood the savage cut which was made at his head, and with his clenched left hand hit his opponent such a blow on the chest as laid him flat on the sand. The man sprang up in an instant, but instead of renewing the attack, to Oliver's surprise he came forward and held out his hand, which the youth was not unwilling to grasp.

"Thank 'ee, sur," he said, somewhat sternly, "you've done me a sarvice; you've prevented me committin' two murders, an' taught me a lesson I never knaw'd afore—that Jim Cuttance an't invulnerable. I don't mind the blow, sur—not I. It wor gov'n in feer fight, an' I was wrang."

"I'm glad to find that you view the matter in that light," said Oliver, with a smile, "and, truly, the blow was given in self-defence by one who will never forget that he owes you his life."

A groan here turned the attention of the party to one of their number who had seated himself on a rock during the foregoing dialogue.

"What! not hurt, are 'ee, Dan?" said his leader, going towards him.

To this Dan replied with another groan, and placed his hand on his hip.

His comrades crowded round him, and, finding that he was wounded and suffering great pain, raised him in their arms and bore him into the cavern, where they laid him on the ground, and, lighting a candle, proceeded to examine him.

"You had better let me look at him, lads," said Oliver, pushing the men gently aside, "I am a surgeon."

They gave place at once, and Oliver soon found that the man had received a pistol-ball in his thigh.

Fortunately it had been turned aside in its course, and lay only a little way beneath the skin, so that it was easily extracted by means of a penknife.

"Now, friends," said Oliver, after completing the dressing of the wound, "before I met with you I had missed my way while travelling to St. Just. Will one of you direct me to the right road, and I shall bid you good night, as I think you have no further need of my services."

The men looked at their leader, whom they evidently expected to be their spokesman.

"Well, sur, you have rendered we some help this hevenin', both in the way o' pickin' out the ball an' helpin' to break skulls as well as preventing worse, so we can do no less than show 'ee the road; but hark 'ee, sur," here the man became very impressive, "ef you do chance to come across any of us in your travels, you had better not knaw us, 'xcept in an or'nary way, d'ye understand? An' us will do the same by thee."

"Of course I will act as you wish," said Oliver, with a smile, "although I do not see why we should be ashamed of this affair, seeing that we were the party attacked. There is only one person to whom I would wish to explain the reason of my not appearing sooner, because he will probably know of the arrival in Penzance this morning of the conveyance that brought me to Cornwall."

"And who may that be?" demanded Jim Cuttance.

"My uncle, Thomas Donnithorne of St. Just," said Oliver.

"Whew!" whistled the fisherman in surprise, while all the others burst into a hearty fit of laughter.

"Why do you laugh?" asked Oliver.

"Oh, never mind, sur, it's all right," said the man with a chuckle. "Iss, you may tell Thomas Donnithorne; there won't be no harm in tellin' he—oh dear no!"

Again the men laughed loud and long, and Oliver felt his powers of forbearance giving way, when Cuttance said to him, "An' you may tell all his friends, too, for they're the right sort. Come now, Maggot here will show 'ee the way up to St. Just."

So saying, the stout fisherman conducted the young surgeon to the mouth of the cavern, and, shaking hands with him, left him to the guidance of the man named Maggot, who led him through several lanes, until he reached the high road between Sennen Church-town and St. Just. Here he paused; told his companion to proceed straight on for about four miles or so, when he would reach the town, and bade him good night.

"And mind 'ee, don't go off the road, sur," shouted Maggot, a few seconds after the young man had left him, "if 'ee don't want to fall down a shaft and scat your skull."

Oliver, not having any desire to scat his skull, whatever that might be, assured the man that he would keep to the road carefully.

The moon shone clear in a cloudless sky, covering the wide moor and the broad Atlantic with a flood of silver light, and rendering the road quite distinct, so that our traveller experienced no further difficulty in pursuing his way. He hurried forward at a rapid pace, yet could not resist the temptation to pause frequently and gaze in admiration on the scene of desolate grandeur around him. On such occasions he found it difficult to believe that the stirring events of the last few hours were real. Indeed, if it had not been that there were certain uneasy portions of his frame—the result of his recent encounter on the beach—which afforded constant and convincing evidence that he was awake, he would have been tempted to believe that the adventures of that day were nothing more than a vivid dream.

J. C. TREGARTHEN
(1854–1933)

You're right, we haven't seen much of the natural world yet, have we? Other than a few birds in Fowey. I know just the person to set us right.

John Coulson Tregarthen was a Penzance-born naturalist who retired from teaching to write books about wildlife – *The Life Story of an Otter*, *The Life Story of a Badger*, *The Life Story of a Fox*, and *The Story of a Hare*. In his preface to the *Otter* he says he hopes the book will 'bring about a wider and deeper interest in the animal'. It certainly did, inspiring fellow writer Henry Williamson to write his own classic, *Tarka the Otter*, some twenty years later.

Be warned, Tregarthen's animal stories are not sentimental. He was a fellow of the Zoological Society of London and his writing is informed by close observation. In each of his animal *Lives* there is a threat hanging over wildlife: the hunt. The following chapter opens with the otter family hunting pike and salmon, but the scene really explodes when the hounds appear.

from The Life Story of an Otter

Sitting there, the cub watched the lurid afterglow fade, dusk creep over the rough water, and the sky darken till a star appeared in a break between the scudding wrack. Then he rose and listened. The waves broke against the point, the reeds hissed, the breakers thundered on the bar, but no call from his mother reached his eager ears. He was beginning to fear she had deserted him when from across the mere came the shrill summons. Immediately he dived and, rising almost at once, headed at excited pace for the creek, where soon, to his delight, he viewed his mother and sister swimming to meet him. The wild gambols that followed in the midst of the mere did not last long, for there was hunting to be done.

The quarry the otter had set her mind on were the pike frequenting the reedy bays, towards the largest of which the hunters swam. Near a bed of lilies they dived, and had not made half the circuit of the wall of stems before they espied a pike. He had already seen them, and in an instant the protruding muzzle was withdrawn as the fish backed into his ambush. It afforded him no refuge from the pursuers, who drove him from one to another of its recesses, and pressed him so closely that, as he saw, to remain meant capture. Out he flashed and, had he made right away and gained the heart of the mere, he would have escaped. But he sought the shelter of another lily-bed almost within sight of the first, and there the otters followed in unrelenting chase. Presently he was gripped by the male cub, but, freeing himself, forsook the weeds for the water outside, where, with distended jaws and fins erect, he darted now here, now there, to avoid his harassing pursuers. All was in vain. He had missed his earlier opportunities, and to escape in his exhausted condition was impossible. Conscious of this and determined not to die unavenged, he summoned his remaining strength, dashed at the otter, seized her by the throat, and held on despite her struggles. This however left him at the mercy of the cubs. Instantly they fastened on his shoulders and, using their powerful rudders, tried to raise him to the surface. Beating his tail, the fish for awhile succeeded in resisting their efforts; but in the end he tired, and presently the writhing mass came to the top of the lake and, rolling over and over, showed now on the crest, now in the trough of the waves. There the otter wrenched herself free and, half-throttled though she was, at once joined in the attack. The three soon overpowered their prey and landed with it at an opening in the reeds. Whilst they were dragging it from the water's edge a tremor passed through the fish. Immediately the hungry hunters relaxed their hold, fell to and sliced and sliced and champed and champed till wellnigh half the fish was eaten and the great backbone showed. The feast over, they licked their chops, brushed their whiskers against the stems and, taking to the water, played hide-and-seek amongst the lilies.

The exultation they felt over their capture showed in their excited gambols and in their wild rush through the reed-bed on their way to the bar. They crossed this at a gallop to the edge of the tide, plunged into the breakers and, reaching the quieter water beyond the surf, headed straight for the great pile of rocks over which the spray was dashing in clouds. On landing, they threaded the sobbing passages between the boulders and gained the caves that honeycomb the cliff behind. There they came on the remains of old feasts—fish bones, crab and lobster shells—and on old nests made of reeds. One cave there was where the muffled boom of the waves was broken by the tinkle of falling water, and where the skeletons of otters whitened the floor on the edge of the runlet that had worn a channel in the rock. Quickly leaving it, the animals made their way back along the low, tortuous passage by which they had entered and, passing through the outer caves, regained the clitter. There they chased one another until they tired. Then they took to the sea, reached the line of the breakers, and landed through the welter as easily as, later, they landed on the bank of the mere by the inflow. The otter was then leading her cubs to the withy-bed and to the boggy ground between it and the old decoy, where she trod the watermint as she went.

So the hours of darkness were spent, and when the grey light told of coming day otter and cubs slipped into the stream and drifted towards the mere. On reaching the choppy water they fell to swimming, turned up the sheltered creek, skirted the island where two of them had kennelled the day before, and landed near a bramble brake, in which they curled up side by side. The cubs soon slept, but the excitement of the journey to the salmon river kept the otter awake longing for dusk, so eager was she to cross the moors and reach the pools. She dropped asleep at last, but awoke long before setting-out time and, whilst awaiting nightfall, watched the angry sun go down and the clouds scud by close overhead.

Before it was quite dark she aroused the cubs, and made up the hilly ground towards the heart of the moor. It was a wild night, but the fury of the gale seemed to quicken the energies of the wanderers, for they breasted the foothills at a pace beyond their wont and soon gained the high plateau with its chain of pools, known to men as the Black Liddens. These they swam as they came to them, passed to the heathery waste with its old Stone Circle, and reached the marshy valley and the lazy stream which supplies the mere. The wind had little force there—the thorns, shaggy with lichen, stood motionless, even the bulrushes scarcely stirred; but over a stagnant backwater a will-o'-the-wisp kept dancing like a lantern swung by invisible hands. Splash! splash! the otters crossed the shallow pool near the stream; and again, splash! splash! they rushed through the shoal water beyond it before turning up the brae that led to the windswept moor. On, on the untiring creatures sped, more like agents of darkness executing some urgent commission than beasts of prey speeding to a new fishing-ground. Mile after mile of the desolate upland they traversed: at one spot skirting a cairn whence came that weirdest of all wild cries, the shrill chattering of badgers; at another, passing the only road over the moor, where they left their footprints between the fresh wheel-marks of the doctor's trap. A sleeping hamlet rose almost in their path, and so close did they approach that they heard the creaking of the signboard of the Druid's Arms, about which the cottages cluster. Then over wall after wall they clambered as they came to the crofters' holdings, reached the lodge of the keeper who had been the otter's terror when her cubs were helpless, gained the edge of the moorland above the old nursery, made their way down the very gully along which the hounds had followed the fox and, leaping the stream close to the hover, came out on the salmon pool beyond the poplar.

Eager to see whether the pool held a fish, the otter slipped into the water and swam to the favourite lie near the foot of the fall. A salmon was there, and towards it she advanced so swiftly that it seemed she must fasten before it could become aware of her presence. But the fish had been harried by otters on its way up from the estuary, and was prepared for her coming. In a flash he was off downstream, leaving the otters far in his wake. At the tail of the pool he swung round, raising a big wave that greatly excited the cubs where they watched on the edge of the bank. After a short interval the wave came again, and again, and again. Later the salmon leapt clear of the white water near the fall. And so the chase continued, until the otter, seeing how vain were her unaided efforts, summoned the cubs to her assistance. In an instant they slipped into the pool and joined in the pursuit.

Now wherever the salmon turns an otter meets him. Conscious of the danger he is in, he rushes at the shallows in a daring attempt to reach the waters below. His three enemies hurry after him, breaking the surface in their desperate haste, and while he is still floundering the otter closes and strives to grip him beneath the gills. No defence has he but his slippery scales and the lashing tail that sweeps his foes aside. But these avail, and before the teeth fasten in him he struggles through to the deep water beyond, where he easily outdistances his pursuers. Pool after pool he passes at his utmost speed, making for a refuge that lies near the foot of the rapids. He had rested in it on his way up the river, and now swings into it and stays there gasping, in dread of discovery. The otters soon show on the top of the rushing waters, which they search as they descend, ducking their heads, and yet avoiding the rocks against which the current threatens to dash them. In a few seconds they are close to the spot where the fish lies exhausted, and surely one or other will get a glimpse of him. But no, the sheltering rock befriends him, or the foaming waters amidst which he lies. The hunters pass on; but he is not safe yet. If they draw the rapids against the stream they can hardly miss him. But will they? Apparently not—at least, not for the moment. They are going on, despite the near approach of day. How carefully they examine the hollow banks and recesses of the boulders, disdaining even the grilse they disturb, in their expectation of yet getting the salmon! Beneath the gloomy pines that form a vista towards the brightening east they swim, eager as ever.

But, clear of the trees, they all at once cease their quest and listen. Some suspicious sound downstream has alarmed them. They are all ears when, above the voice of the river and the wild rustling of the tree-tops, the penetrating note again makes itself heard. It is the toot of the horn. The twice-hunted otter dreads that sound above all sounds save the cry of the hounds, and before it has died away she and the cubs are in full retreat to the holt in the salmon pool. Only at long intervals do they rise to vent before reaching the rapids, where they leave the water and gallop up the bank, as if fear itself were at their heels. At the top they re-enter the river, and so gain the shelter of the alder-roots near the fall.

The cubs, feeling safe in the holt, make their toilet as usual; but the otter listens, and before long catches the dreaded cry. Then the cubs hear it too: they begin to share their mother's alarm and, when the swelling clamour tells of the close approach of their enemies, seek the inmost recess of their refuge. Soon the hounds enter the pool and cluster like maddened things about the holt. 'A good solid mark,' shouts the doctor to the squire. 'He's there right enough.' The foremost hounds can see the otter where she stands hissing through her white teeth, but they cannot reach her. So the hounds are called off that a terrier may get at the quarry, and after a terrible fight he compels the otter to take to the water. Shouts of

'Heu gaz' from the field greet the appearance of the bubbles that betray her flight, and the next moment the twelve couple of hounds are in pursuit towards the stickle, where a dozen men or more stand foot to foot to prevent her from going down-water. Round and round the big pool swims the otter, rising now under the bank, now amongst the hounds, narrowly escaping their jaws. Time after time she returns to the cubs, but only to be ejected by one or other of the terriers. At last, after being badly shaken by the hounds, she lands, gallops round the line of men with the white terrier at her rudder, and gains the water beyond. At amazing speed she follows the winding reaches to the rapids, and even succeeds in gaining Longen Pool, famous in the annals of the Hunt. However, the hounds again press her sorely, and after a while she takes to the tangled coppice on the hillside, traverses it, reaches an ancient hedgerow matted with bramble and thorn, and there lies listening, trusting to have escaped pursuit. But she has left a burning scent, and soon the cry of the pursuers warns her that her hopes are vain. Nevertheless, as she is very weary, and as the pool to which the hedge runs down offers no harbourage, she remains where she is. But though the hounds soon wind her, the denseness of the thicket hinders them from getting at her until the terriers force her to the river. In the shallow water every eye can mark her where she swims and note her shortening dives. The end is near. Presently Dosmary seizes her as she rises, and the pack worries her life out.

That night, when the storm had passed, the miller

heard the cries of two otters in the tangled coppice beyond the orchard, and as he knocked the ashes from his pipe before going indoors, said: 'They're missin' her, I'm thinkin'.' He was right. It was the voice of the cubs calling for their mother.

THE GIANTS OF CORNWALL

We've had some trouble with giants in the past, that's for certain – eating children, bothering saints, tossing boulders. For sport, one of them used to reach out over the sea and pick up sailors with his hands, replacing them on the wrong ships. That's how big they were, some of them. They're especially prevalent here in the west of Cornwall, where you can still see evidence of their furniture, games and footprints in the landscape. St Michael's Mount itself is said to have been built by the giant Cormoran.

As a warning, then, here are a few old tales of the giants and their deeds, and of the heroes who came to squash them. We'll begin at the beginning, with Corineus, one of the first kings of Cornwall, who arrived with the Trojan Brutus – the chap said to have given his name to Britain.

When they landed, Corineus was gifted Cornwall, a place so riddled with giants that both St Agnes and Jack the Giant Killer were still mopping them up many centuries later.

from Histories of the Kings of Britain
and the Origins of Cornwall
by Geoffrey of Monmouth

At that time the name of the island was Albion, and of none was it inhabited save only of a few giants. Natheless the pleasant aspect of the land, with the abundance of fish in the rivers and deer in the choice forests thereof did fill Brute and his companions with no small desire that they should dwell therein. Wherefore, after exploring certain districts of the land, they drove the giants they found to take refuge in the caverns of the mountains, and divided the country among them by lot according as the Duke made grant thereof. They begin to till the fields, and to build them houses in such sort that after a brief space ye might have thought it had been inhabited from time immemorial. Then, at last, Brute calleth the island Britain, and his companions Britons, after his own name, for he was minded that his memory should be perpetuated in the derivation of the name. Whence afterward the country speech, which was aforetime called Trojan or crooked Greek, was called British. But Corineus called that share of the kingdom which had fallen unto him by lot Cornwall, after the manner of his own name, and the people Cornishmen, therein following the Duke's example. For albeit that he might have had the choice of a province before all the others that had come thither, yet was he minded rather to have that share of the land which is now called Cornwall, whether from being, as it is, the *cornu* or horn of Britain, or from a corruption of the said name Corineus. For nought gave him greater pleasure than to wrestle with the giants, of whom was greater plenty there than in any of the provinces that had been shared amongst his comrades. Among others was a certain hateful one by name Goemagot, twelve cubits in height, who was of such lustihood, that when he had once uprooted it, he would wield an oak tree as lightly as it were a wand of hazel. On a certain day when Brute was holding high festival to the gods in the port whereat he had first landed, this one, along with a score other giants, fell upon him and did passing cruel slaughter on the British. Howbeit, at the last, the Britons collecting together from all quarters prevailed against them and slew them all, save Goemagot only. Him Brute had commanded to be kept alive, as he was minded to see a wrestling bout betwixt him and Corineus, who was beyond measure keen to match himself against such monsters. So Corineus, overjoyed at the prospect, girt himself for the encounter, and flinging away his arms, challenged him to a bout at wrestling. At the start, on the one side stands Corineus, on the other the giant, each hugging the other tight in the shackles of their arms, both making the very air quake with their breathless gasping. It was not long before Goemagot, grasping Corineus with all his force, brake him three of his ribs, two on the right side and one on the left. Roused thereby to fury, Corineus gathered up all his strength, heaved him up on his shoulders and ran with his burden as fast as he could for the weight to the sea-shore nighest at hand. Mounting up to the top of a high cliff, and disengaging himself, he hurled the deadly monster he had carried on his shoulder into the sea, where, falling on the sharp rocks, he was mangled all to pieces and dyed the waves with his blood, so that ever thereafter that place from the flinging down of the giant hath been known as Lamgoemagot, to wit, 'Goemagot's Leap,' and is called by that name unto this present day.

from 'The Giant Bolster' by Robert Hunt

Bolster must have been of enormous size: since it is stated that he could stand with one foot on St Agnes' Beacon and the other on Carn Brea; these hills being distant, as the bird flies, six miles, his immensity will be clear to all. In proof of this, there still exists, in the valley running upwards from Chapel Porth, a stone in which may yet be seen the impression of the giant's fingers. On one occasion, Bolster, when enjoying his usual stride from the Beacon to Carn Brea, felt thirsty, and stooped to drink out of the well at Chapel Porth, resting, while he did so, on the above-mentioned stone. We hear but little of the wives of our giants; but Bolster had a wife, who was made to labour hard by her tyrannical husband. On the top of St Agnes' Beacon there yet exist the evidences of the useless labours to which this unfortunate giantess was doomed, in grouped masses of small stones. These, it is said, have all been gathered from an estate at the foot of the hill, immediately adjoining the village of St Agnes. This farm is to the present day remarkable for its freedom from stones, though situated amidst several others, which, like most lands reclaimed from the moors of this district, have stones in abundance mixed with the soil. Whenever Bolster was angry with his wife, he compelled her to pick stones, and to carry them in her apron to the top of the hill. There is some confusion in the history of this giant, and of the

154

blessed St Agnes to whom the church is dedicated. They are supposed to have lived at the same time, which, according to our views, is scarcely probable, believing, as we do, that no giants existed long after their defeat at Plymouth by Brutus and Corineus. There may have been an earlier saint of the same name; or may not Saint Enns or Anns, the popular name of this parish, indicate some other lady?

Be this as it may, the giant Bolster became deeply in love with St Agnes, who is reputed to have been singularly beautiful, and a pattern woman of virtue. The giant allowed the lady no repose. He followed her incessantly, proclaiming his love, and filling the air with the tempests of his sighs and groans. St Agnes lectured Bolster in vain on the impropriety of his conduct, he being already a married man. This availed not; her prayers to him to relieve her from his importunities were also in vain. The persecuted lady, finding there was no release for her, while this monster existed, resolved to be rid of him at any cost, and eventually succeeded by the following stratagem:—Agnes appeared at length to be persuaded of the intensity of the giant's love, but she told him she required yet one small proof more. There exists at Chapel Porth a hole in the cliff at the termination of the valley. If Bolster would fill this hole with his blood the lady would no longer look coldly on him. This huge bestrider-of-the-hills thought that it was an easy thing which was required of him, and felt that he could fill many such holes and be none the weaker for the loss of blood. Consequently, stretching his great arm across the hole, he plunged a knife into a vein, and a torrent of gore issued forth. Roaring and seething the blood fell to the bottom, and the giant expected in a few minutes to see the test of his devotion made evident, in the filling of the hole. It required much more blood than Bolster had supposed; still it must in a short time be filled, so he bled on. Hour after hour the blood flowed from the vein, yet the hole was not filled. Eventually the giant fainted from exhaustion. The strength of life within his mighty frame enabled him to rally, yet he had no power to lift himself from the ground, and he was unable to stanch the wound which he had made. Thus it was, that after many throes, the giant Bolster died!

The cunning saint, in proposing this task to Bolster, was well aware that the hole opened at the bottom into the sea, and that as rapidly as the blood flowed into the hole it ran from it, and did

"The multitudinous seas incarnadine,
Making the green one red."

Thus the lady got rid of her hated lover; Mrs Bolster was released, and the district freed from the presence of a tyrant. The hole at Chapel Porth still retains the evidences of the truth of this tradition, in the red stain which marks the track down which flowed the giant's blood.

from 'Jack the Giant Killer'
by James Orchard Halliwell-Phillipps

In the reign of King Arthur, and in the county of Cornwall, near to the Land's End of England, there lived a wealthy farmer, who had an only son named Jack. He was brisk, and of a lively ready wit, so that whatever he could not perform by force and strength, he accomplished by ingenious wit and policy. Never was any person heard of that could worst him, and he very often even baffled the learned by his sharp and ready inventions.

In those days the Mount of Cornwall was kept by a huge and monstrous giant of eighteen feet in height, and about three yards in compass, of a fierce and grim countenance, the terror of all the neighbouring towns and villages. He inhabited a cave in the middle of the mount, and he was such a selfish monster that he would not suffer any one to live near him. He fed on other men's cattle, which often became his prey, for whensoever he wanted food, he would wade over to the main land, where he would furnish himself with whatever came in his way. The inhabitants, at his approach, forsook their habitations, while he seized on their cattle, making nothing of carrying half-a-dozen oxen on his back at a time; and as for their sheep and hogs, he would tie them round his waist like a bunch of bandoleers. This course he had followed for many years, so that a great part of the county was impoverished by his depredations.

This was the state of affairs, when Jack, happening one day to be present at the town-hall when the authorities were consulting about the giant, had the curiosity to ask what reward would be given to the person who destroyed him. The giant's treasure was declared as the recompense, and Jack at once undertook the task.

In order to accomplish his purpose, he furnished himself with a horn, shovel, and pickaxe, and went over to the Mount in the beginning of a dark winter's evening, when he fell to work, and before morning had dug a pit twenty-two feet deep, and nearly as broad, covering it over with long sticks and straw. Then strewing a little mould upon it, it appeared like plain ground. This accomplished, Jack placed himself on the side of the pit which was furthest from the giant's lodging, and, just at the break of day, he put the horn to his mouth, and blew with all his might. Although Jack was a little fellow, and the powers of his voice are not described as being very great, he managed to make noise enough to arouse the giant, and excite his indignation. The monster accordingly rushed from his cave, exclaiming, "You incorrigible villain, are you come here to disturb my rest? you shall pay dearly for this. Satisfaction I will have, for I will take you whole and broil you for breakfast." He had no sooner uttered this cruel threat, than tumbling into the pit, he made the very foundations of the Mount ring again. "Oh, giant," said Jack, "where are you now? Oh faith, you are gotten now into Lob's Pound, where I will surely plague you for your threatening words: what do you think now of broiling me for your breakfast? will no other diet serve you but poor Jack?" Thus did little Jack tantalize the big giant, as a cat does a mouse when she knows it cannot escape, and when he had tired of that amusement, he gave him a heavy blow with his pickaxe on the very crown of his head, which "tumbled him down," and killed him on the spot. When Jack saw he was dead, he filled up the pit with earth, and went to search the cave, which he found contained much treasure. The magistrates, in the exuberance of their joy, did not add to Jack's gains from their own, but after the best and cheapest mode of payment, made a declaration he should henceforth be termed *Jack the Giant-killer,* and presented him with a sword and embroidered belt, on the latter of which were inscribed these words in letters of gold:

> Here's the right valiant Cornish man,
> Who slew the giant Cormelian.

The news of Jack's victory, as might be expected, soon spread over all the West of England, so that another giant, named Thunderbore, hearing of it, and entertaining a partiality for his race, vowed to be revenged on the little hero, if ever it was his fortune to light on him. This giant was the lord of an enchanted castle, situated in the midst of a lonely wood. Now Jack, about four months after his last exploit, walking near this castle in his journey towards Wales, being weary, seated himself near a pleasant fountain in the wood, "o'ercanopied with luscious woodbine," and presently fell asleep. While he was enjoying his repose, the giant, coming to the fountain for water, of course discovered him, and recognised the hated individual by the lines written on the belt. He immediately took Jack on his shoulders, and carried him towards his enchanted castle. Now, as they passed through a thicket, the rustling of the boughs awakened Jack, who was uncomfortably surprised to find himself in the clutches of the giant. His terror was not diminished when, on entering the castle, he saw the court-yard strewed with human bones, the giant maliciously telling him his own would ere long increase the hateful pile. After this assurance, the cannibal locked poor Jack in an upper chamber, leaving him there while he went to fetch another giant living in the same wood to keep him company in the anticipated destruction of their enemy. While he was gone, dreadful shrieks and lamentations affrighted Jack, especially a voice which continually cried,—

> Do what you can to get away,
> Or you'll become the giant's prey;
> He's gone to fetch his brother, who
> Will kill, and likewise torture you.

This warning, and the hideous tone in which it was delivered, almost distracted poor Jack, who going to the window, and opening a casement, beheld afar off the two giants approaching towards the castle. "Now," quoth Jack to himself, "my death or my deliverance is at hand." The event proved that his anticipations were well founded, for the giants of those days, however powerful, were at best very stupid fellows, and readily conquered by stratagem, were it of the humblest kind. There happened to be strong cords in the room in which Jack was confined, two of which he took, and made a strong noose at the end of each; and while the giant was unlocking the iron gate of the castle, he threw the ropes over each of their heads, and then, before the giants knew what he was about, he drew the other ends across a beam, and, pulling with all his might, throttled them till they were black in the face. Then, sliding down the rope, he came to their heads, and as they could not defend themselves, easily despatched them with his sword. This business so adroitly accomplished, Jack released the fair prisoners in the castle, delivered the keys to them, and, like a true knight-errant, continued his journey without condescending to improve the condition of his purse.

This plan, however honorable, was not without its disadvantages, and owing to his slender stock of money, he was obliged to make the best of his way by travelling as hard as he could. At length, losing his road, he was belated, and could not get to any place of entertainment until, coming to a lonesome valley, he found a large house, and by reason of his present necessity, took courage to knock at the gate. But what was his astonishment, when there came forth a monstrous giant with two heads; yet he did not appear so fiery as the others were, for he was a Welsh giant, and what he did was by private and secret malice under the false show of friendship. Jack having unfolded his condition to the giant, was shown into a bedroom, where, in the dead of night, he heard his host in another apartment uttering these formidable words:

Though here you lodge with me this night,
You shall not see the morning light:
My club shall dash your brains out quite!

"Say'st thou so," quoth Jack; "that is like one of your Welsh tricks, yet I hope to be cunning enough for you." He immediately got out of bed, and, feeling about in the dark, found a thick billet of wood, which he laid in the bed in his stead, and hid himself in a dark corner of the room. Shortly after he had done so, in came the Welsh giant, who thoroughly pummelled the billet with his club, thinking, naturally enough, he had broken every bone in Jack's skin. The next morning, however, to the inexpressible surprise of the giant, Jack came down stairs as if nothing had happened, and gave him thanks for his night's lodging. "How have you rested," quoth the giant; "did you not feel anything in the night?" Jack provokingly replied, "No, nothing but a rat which gave me two or three flaps with her tail." This reply was totally incomprehensible to the giant, who of course saw anything but a joke in it. However, concealing his amazement as well as he could, he took Jack in to breakfast, assigning to each a bowl containing four gallons of hasty pudding. One would have thought that the greater portion of so extravagant an allowance would have been declined by our hero, but he was unwilling the giant should imagine his incapability to eat it, and accordingly placed a large leather bag under his loose coat, in such a position that he could convey the pudding into it without the deception being perceived. Breakfast at length being finished, Jack excited the giant's curiosity by offering to show him an extraordinary sleight of hand; so taking a knife, he ripped the leather bag, and out of course descended on the ground all the hasty pudding. The giant had not the slightest suspicion of the trick, veritably believing the pudding came from its natural receptacle; and having the same antipathy to being beaten, exclaimed in true Welsh, "Odds splutters, hur can do that trick hurself." The sequel may be readily guessed. The monster took the knife, and thinking to follow Jack's example with impunity, killed himself on the spot.

King Arthur's only son requested his father to furnish him with a large sum of money, in order that he might go and seek his fortune in the principality of Wales, where lived a beautiful lady possessed with seven evil spirits. The king tried all he could do to persuade him to alter his determination, but it was all in vain, so at last he granted his request, and the prince set out with two horses, one loaded with money, the other for himself to ride upon. Now, after several days' travel, he came to a market-town in Wales, where he beheld a vast concourse of people gathered together. The prince demanded the reason of it, and was told that they had arrested a corpse for several large sums of money which the deceased owed when he died. The prince replied that it was a pity creditors should be so cruel, and said, "Go bury the dead, and let his creditors come to my lodging, and there their debts shall be discharged." They accordingly came, but in such great numbers, that before night he had almost left himself penniless.

Now Jack the Giant-killer happened to be in the town while these transactions took place, and he was so pleased with the generosity exhibited by the prince, that he offered to become his servant, an offer which was immediately accepted. The next morning they set forward on their journey, when, as they were just leaving the town, an old woman called after the prince, saying, "He has owed me twopence these seven years; pray pay me as well as the rest." So reasonable and urgent a demand could not be resisted, and the prince immediately discharged the debt, but it took the last penny he had to accomplish it. This event, though generally ridiculed by heroes, was one by no means overlooked by the prince, who required all Jack's assuring eloquence to console him. Jack himself, indeed, had a very poor exchequer, and after their day's refreshment, they were entirely without money. When night drew on, the prince was anxious to secure a lodging, but as they had no means to hire one, Jack said, "Never mind, master, we shall do well enough, for I have an uncle lives within two miles of this place; he is a huge and monstrous giant with three heads; he'll fight five hundred men in armour, and make them flee before him." "Alas!" quoth the prince, "what shall we do there? He'll certainly chop us up at a mouthful. Nay, we are scarce enough to fill his hollow tooth!" "It is no matter for that," quoth Jack; "I myself will go before, and prepare the way for you; therefore tarry and wait till I return." Jack then rides off full speed, and coming to the gate of the castle, he knocked so loud that the neighbouring hills resounded like thunder. The giant, terribly vexed with the liberty taken by Jack, roared out, "Who's there?" He was answered, "None but your poor cousin Jack." Quoth he, "What news with my poor cousin Jack?" He replied, "Dear uncle, heavy news." "God wot," quoth the giant, "prithee what heavy news can come to me? I am a giant with three heads, and besides thou knowest I can fight five hundred men in armour, and make them fly like chaff before the wind." "Oh, but," quoth Jack, "here's the prince a-coming with a thousand men in armour to kill you, and destroy all that you have!" "Oh, cousin Jack," said the giant, "this is heavy news indeed! I will immediately run and hide myself, and thou shalt lock, bolt, and bar me in, and keep the keys till the prince is gone." Jack joyfully complied with the giant's request, and fetching his master, they feasted and made themselves merry whilst the poor giant laid trembling in a vault under ground.

In the morning, Jack furnished the prince with a fresh supply of gold and silver, and then sent him three miles forward on his journey, concluding, according to the story-book, "he was then pretty well out of the smell of the giant." Jack afterwards returned, and liberated the giant from the vault, who asked what he should give him for preserving the castle from destruction. "Why," quoth Jack, "I desire nothing but the old coat and cap, together with the old rusty sword and slippers which are at your bed's head." Quoth the giant, "Thou shalt have them, and pray keep them for my sake, for they are things of excellent use; the coat will keep you invisible, the cap will furnish you with knowledge, the sword cuts asunder whatever you strike, and the shoes are of extraordinary swiftness. These may be serviceable to you: therefore take them with all my heart."

Jack was delighted with these useful presents, and having overtaken his master, they quickly arrived at the lady's house, who, finding the prince to be a suitor, prepared a splendid banquet for him. After the repast was concluded, she wiped his mouth with a handkerchief, and then concealed it in her dress, saying, "You must show me that handkerchief to-morrow morning, or else you will lose your head." The prince went to bed in great sorrow at this hard condition, but fortunately Jack's cap of knowledge instructed him how it was to be fulfilled. In the middle of the night she called upon her familiar to carry her to the evil spirit. Jack immediately put on his coat of darkness, and his shoes of swiftness, and was there before her, his coat rendering him invisible. When she entered the lower regions, she gave the handkerchief to the spirit, who laid it upon a shelf, whence Jack took it, and brought it to his master, who showed it to the lady the next day, and so saved his life. The next evening at supper she saluted the prince, telling him he must show her the lips tomorrow morning that she kissed last this night, or lose his head. He replied, "If you kiss none

166

but mine, I will." "That is neither here nor there," said she, "if you do not, death is your portion!" At midnight she went below as before, and was angry with the spirit for letting the handkerchief go: "But now," quoth she, "I will be too hard for the prince, for I will kiss thee, and he is to show me thy lips." She did so, and Jack, who was standing by, cut off the spirit's head, and brought it under his invisible coat to his master, who produced it triumphantly the next morning before the lady. This feat destroyed the enchantment, the evil spirits immediately forsook her, and she appeared still more sweet and lovely, beautiful as she was before. They were married the next morning, and shortly afterwards went to the court of King Arthur, where Jack, for his eminent services, was created one of the knights of the Round Table.

Our hero, having been successful in all his undertakings, and resolving not to remain idle, but to perform what services he could for the honour of his country, humbly besought his majesty to fit him out with a horse and money to enable him to travel in search of new adventures; for, said he, "there are many giants yet living in the remote part of Wales, to the unspeakable damage of your majesty's subjects; wherefore may it please you to encourage me, I do not doubt but in a short time to cut them off root and branch, and so rid all the realm of those giants and monsters in human shape." We need scarcely say that Jack's generous offer was at once accepted. The king furnished him with the necessary accoutrements, and Jack set out with his magical cap, sword, and shoes, the better to perform the dangerous enterprises which now lay before him.

After travelling over several hills and mountains, the country through which he passed offering many impediments to travellers, on the third day he arrived at a very large wood, which he had no sooner entered than his ears were assailed with piercing shrieks. Advancing softly towards the place where the cries appeared to proceed from, he was horror-struck at perceiving a huge giant dragging along a fair lady, and a knight her husband, by the hair of their heads, "with as much ease," says the original narrative, "as if they had been a pair of gloves." Jack shed tears of pity on the fate of this hapless couple, but not suffering his feelings to render him neglectful of action, he put on his invisible coat, and taking with him his infallible sword, succeeded, after considerable trouble, and many cuts, to despatch the monster, whose dying groans were so terrible, that they made the whole wood ring again. The courteous knight and his fair lady were overpowered with gratitude, and, after returning Jack their best thanks, they invited him to their residence, there to recruit his strength after the frightful encounter, and receive more substantial demonstrations of their obligations to him. Jack, however, declared that he would not rest until he had found out the giant's habitation. The knight, on hearing this determination, was very sorrowful, and replied, "Noble stranger, it is too much to run a second hazard: this monster lived in a den under yonder mountain, with a brother more fierce and cruel than himself. Therefore, if you should go thither, and perish in the attempt, it would be a heart-breaking to me and my lady: let me persuade you to go with us, and desist from any further pursuit." The knight's reasoning had the very opposite effect that was intended, for Jack, hearing of another giant, eagerly embraced the opportunity of displaying his skill, promising, however, to return to the knight when he had accomplished his second labour.

He had not ridden more than a mile and a half, when the cave mentioned by the knight appeared to view, near the entrance of which he beheld the giant, sitting upon a block of timber, with a knotted iron club by his side, waiting, as he supposed, for his brother's return with his barbarous prey. This giant is described as having "goggle eyes like flames of fire, a countenance grim and ugly, cheeks like a couple of large flitches of bacon, the bristles of his beard resembling rods of iron wire, and locks that hung down upon his brawny shoulders like curled snakes or hissing adders." Jack alighted from his horse, and putting on the invisible coat, approached near the giant, and said softly, "Oh! are you there? it will not be long ere I shall take you fast by the beard." The giant all this while could not see him, on account of his invisible coat, so that Jack, coming up close to the monster, struck a blow with his sword at his head, but unfortunately missing his aim, he cut off the nose instead. The giant, as we may suppose, "roared like claps of thunder," and began to lay about him in all directions with his iron club so desperately, that even Jack was frightened, but exercising his usual ingenuity, he soon despatched him.

After this, Jack cut off the giant's head, and sent it, together with that of his brother, to King Arthur, by a waggoner he hired for that purpose, who gave an account of all his wonderful proceedings.

The redoubtable Jack next proceeded to search the giant's cave in search of his treasure, and passing along through a great many winding passages, he came at length to a large room paved with freestone, at the upper end of which was a boiling caldron, and on the right hand a large table, at which the giants usually dined. After passing this dining-room, he came to a large and well-secured den filled with human captives, who were fattened and taken at intervals for food, as we do poultry. Jack set the poor prisoners at liberty, and, to compensate them for their sufferings and dreadful anticipations, shared the giant's treasure equally amongst them, and sent them to their homes overjoyed at their unexpected deliverance.

It was about sunrise when Jack, after the conclusion of this adventure, having had a good night's rest, mounted his horse to proceed on his journey, and, by the help of directions, reached the knight's house about noon. He was received with the most extraordinary demonstrations of joy, and his kind host, out of respect to Jack, prepared a feast which lasted many days, all the nobility and gentry in the neighbourhood being invited to it. The knight related the hero's adventures to his assembled guests, and presented him with a beautiful ring, on which was engraved a representation of the giant dragging the distressed knight and his lady, with this motto:

> We were in sad distress you see,
>   Under the giant's fierce command,
> But gain'd our lives and liberty
>   By valiant Jack's victorious hand.

But earthly happiness is not generally of long duration, and so in some respects it proved on the present occasion, for in the midst of the festivities arrived a messenger with the dismal intelligence that one Thunderdell, a giant with two heads, having heard of the death of his two kinsmen, came from the north to be revenged on Jack, and was already within a mile of the knight's house, the country people flying before him in all directions. The intelligence had no effect on the dauntless Jack, who immediately said, "Let him come! I have a tool to pick his teeth;" and with this elegant assertion, he invited the guests to witness his performance from a high terrace in the garden of the castle.

It is now necessary to inform the reader that the knight's house or castle was situated in an island encompassed with a moat thirty feet deep, and twenty feet wide, passable by a drawbridge. Now Jack, intending to accomplish his purpose by a clever stratagem, employed men to cut through this drawbridge on both sides nearly to the middle; and then, dressing himself in his invisible coat, he marched against the giant with his well-tried sword. As he approached his adversary, although invisible, the giant, being, as it appears, an epicure in such matters, was aware of his approach, and exclaimed, in a fearful tone of voice—

Fi, fee, fo, fum!
I smell the blood of an English man!
Be he alive or be he dead,
I'll grind his bones to make me bread!

"Say you so," said Jack; "then you are a monstrous miller indeed." The giant, deeply incensed, replied, "Art thou that villain who killed my kinsman? then I will tear thee with my teeth, and grind thy bones to powder." "But," says Jack, still provoking him, "you must catch me first, if you please:" so putting aside his invisible coat, so that the giant might see him, and putting on his wonderful shoes, he enticed him into a chase by just approaching near enough to give him an apparent chance of capture. The giant, we are told, "followed like a walking castle, so that the very foundations of the earth seemed to shake at every step." Jack led him a good distance, in order that the wondering guests at the castle might see him to advantage, but at last, to end the matter, he ran over the drawbridge, the giant pursuing him with his club; but coming to the place where the bridge was cut, the giant's great weight burst it asunder, and he was precipitated into the moat, where he rolled about, says the author, "like a vast whale." While the monster was in this condition, Jack sadly bantered him about the boast he had made of grinding his bones to powder, but at length, having teased him sufficiently, a cart-rope was cast over the two heads of the giant, and he was drawn ashore by a team of horses, where Jack served him as he had done his relatives, cut off his heads, and sent them to King Arthur.

It would seem that the giant-killer rested a short time after this adventure, but he was soon tired of inactivity, and again went in search of another giant, the last whose head he was destined to chop off. After passing a long distance, he came at length to a large mountain, at the foot of which was a very lonely house. Knocking at the door, it was opened by "an ancient man, with a head as white as snow," who received Jack very courteously, and at once consented to his request for a lodging. Whilst they were at supper, the old man, who appears to have known more than was suspected, thus addressed the hero: "Son, I am sensible you are a conqueror of giants, and I therefore inform you that on the top of this mountain is an enchanted castle, maintained by a giant named Galligantus, who, by the help of a conjuror, gets many knights into his castle, where they are transformed into sundry shapes and forms: but, above all, I especially lament a duke's daughter, whom they took from her father's garden, bringing her through the air in a chariot drawn by fiery dragons, and securing her within the castle walls, transformed her into the shape of a hind. Now, though a great many knights have endeavoured to break the enchantment, and work her deliverance, yet no one has been able to accomplish it, on account of two fiery griffins which are placed at the gate, and which destroyed them at their approach; but you, my son, being furnished with an invisible coat, may pass by them undiscovered, and on the gates of the castle you will find engraven in large characters by what means the enchantment may be broken." The undaunted Jack at once accepted the commission, and pledged his faith to the old man to proceed early in the morning on this new adventure.

In the morning, as soon as it was daylight, Jack put on his invisible coat, and prepared himself for the enterprise. When he had reached the top of the mountain, he discovered the two fiery griffins, but, being invisible, he passed them without the slightest danger. When he had reached the gate of the castle, he noticed a golden trumpet attached to it, under which were written in large characters the following lines:

> Whoever doth this trumpet blow,
> Shall soon the giant overthrow,
> And break the black enchantment straight,
> So all shall be in happy state.

Jack at once accepted the challenge, and putting the trumpet to his mouth, gave a blast that made the hills re-echo. The castle trembled to its foundations, and the giant and conjuror were overstricken with fear, knowing that the reign of their enchantments was at an end. The former was speedily slain by Jack, but the conjuror, mounting up into the air, was carried away in a whirlwind, and never heard of more. The enchantments were immediately broken, and all the lords and ladies, who had so long been cruelly transformed, were standing on the native earth in their natural shapes, the castle having vanished with the conjuror.

The only relic of the giant which was left was the head, which Jack cut off in the first instance, and which we must suppose rolled away from the influence of the enchanted castle, or it would have "vanished into thin air" with the body. It was fortunate that it did so, for it proved an inestimable trophy at the court of King Arthur, where Jack the Giant-killer was shortly afterwards united to the duke's daughter whom he had freed from enchantment, "not only to the joy of the court, but of all the kingdom." To complete his happiness, he was endowed with a noble house and estates, and his *penchant* for giant-killing having subsided, or, what is more probable, no more monsters appearing to interrupt his tranquillity, he accomplished the usual conclusion to these romantic narratives, by passing the remainder of his life in the enjoyment of every domestic felicity.

D. H. LAWRENCE
(1885–1930)

Frieda and D. H. Lawrence didn't quite fit in. They'd fled wartime London for Cornwall, staying at Porthcothan before heading west to Tregerthen, Zennor. Perhaps they made the mistake of thinking Cornwall was some sort of remote, peaceful retreat.

Frieda wrote about their early days in Zennor as idyllic, while Lawrence was relieved to have left 'English London', as he called it. They invited other artists to join them, like writer Katherine Mansfield and composer Peter Warlock, and Lawrence befriended the local farmer and his sons. But Lawrence was irascible and unconventional and Frieda was German, a combination that led to suspicion during wartime, then harassment, until the police told them to leave.

The retreat became a nightmare, which is how we find it in the autobiographical novel *Kangaroo*. The novel is set in Australia but in the middle of it the main character, Richard Lovat Somers, reflects back to his wartime in Cornwall. It is fair to say Lawrence did not look back altogether fondly.

from Kangaroo

The war-wave had broken right over England, now: right over Cornwall. Probably throughout the ages Cornwall had not been finally swept, submerged by any English spirit. Now it happened—the accursed later war spirit. Now the tales began to go round full-tilt against Somers. A chimney of his house was tarred to keep out the damp: that was a signal to the Germans. He and his wife carried food to supply German submarines. They had secret stores of petrol in the cliff. They were watched and listened to, spied on, by men lying behind the low stone fences. It is a job the Cornish loved. They didn't even mind being caught at it: lying behind a fence with field-glasses, watching through a hole in the drystone wall a man with a lass, on the edge of the moors. Perhaps they were proud of it. If a man wanted to hear what was said about him—or anything—he lay behind a wall at the field-corners, where the youths talked before they parted and went indoors, late of a Saturday night. A whole intense life of spying going on all the time.

Harriet could not hang out a towel on a bush, or carry out the slops, in the empty landscape of moors and sea, without her every movement being followed by invisible eyes. And at evening, when the doors were shut, valiant men lay under the windows to listen to the conversation in the cosy little room. And bitter enough were the things they said: and damnatory, the two Somers.

Richard did not hold himself in. And he talked too with the men on the farm: openly. For they had exactly the same anti-military feeling as himself, and they simply loathed the thought of being compelled to serve. Most men in the west, Somers thought, would have committed murder to escape, if murder would have helped them. It wouldn't. He loved the people at the farm, and the men kindled their rage together. And again Somers' farmer friend warned him, how he was being watched. But Somers *would* not heed. "What can they do to me!" he said. "I am not a spy in any way whatsoever. There is nothing they can do to me. I make no public appearance at all. I am just by myself. What can they do to me? Let them go to hell."

He refused to be watchful, guarded, furtive, like the people around, saying double things as occasion arose, and hiding their secret thoughts and secret malignancy. He still believed in the freedom of the individual.—Yes, freedom of the individual!

He was aware of the mass of secret feeling against him. Yet the people he came into daily contact with liked him—almost loved him. So he kept on defying the rest, and went along blithe and open as ever, saying what he really felt, or holding his tongue. Enemies! How could he have any *personal* enemies? He had never done harm to any of these people, had never even felt any harm. He did not believe in personal enemies. It was just the military.

Enemies he had, however, people he didn't know and hadn't even spoken to. Enemies who hated him like poison. They hated him because he was free, because of his different, unafraid face. They hated him because he wasn't cowed, as they were all cowed. They hated him for his intimacy at the farm, in the hamlet. For each farm was bitter jealous of each other.

Yet he never believed he had any *personal* enemies. And he had all the west hating him like poison. He realised once, when two men came down the moorland by-road—officers in khaki—on a motor-bicycle, and went trying the door of the next cottage, which was shut up. Somers went to the door, in all simplicity.

"Did you want me?" he asked.

"No, we didn't want *you*," replied one of the fellows, in a genteel voice and a tone like a slap in the face. Somers spoken to as if he were the lowest of the low. He shut his cottage door. Was it so? Had they wilfully spoken to him like that? He would not believe it.

But inwardly, he knew it was so. That was what they intended to convey to him: that he was the lowest of the low. He began even to feel guilty, under this mass of poisonous condemnation. And he realised that they had come, on their own, to get into the other cottage and see if there were some wireless installation or something else criminal. But it was fastened tight, and apparently they gave up their design of breaking in, for they turned the motor-cycle and went away.

Day followed day in this tension of suspense. Submarines were off the coast; Harriet saw a ship sunk, away to sea. Horrible excitement, and the postman asking sly questions to try to catch Somers out. Increased rigour of coast watching, and *no* light must be shown. Yet along the highroad on the hillside above, plainer than any house-light, danced the lights of a cart, moving, or slowly sped the light of a bicycle, on the blackness. Then a Spanish coal-vessel, three thousand tons, ran on the rocks in a fog, straight under the cottage. She was completely wrecked. Somers watched the waves break over her. Her coal washed ashore, and the farmers carried it up the cliffs in sacks.

There was to be a calling-up now and a re-examination of every man—Somers felt the crisis approaching. The ordeal was to go through, once more. The first rejection meant nothing. There were certain reservations. He had himself examined again by a doctor. The strain told on his heart as well as his breathing. He sent in this note to the authorities. A reply: "You must present yourself for examination, as ordered."

He knew that if he was really ever summoned to any service, and finally violated, he would be broken, and die.

[...]

Yes—he had his papers—he must present himself again at Bodmin barracks. He was just simply summoned as if he were already conscripted. But he knew he must be medically examined. He went—left home at seven in the morning to catch the train. Harriet watched him go across the field. She was left alone, in a strange country.

"I shall be back to-night," he said.

It was a still morning, remote, as if one were not in

the world. On the hill down to the station he lingered. "Shall I not go! Shall I not go!" he said to himself. He wanted to break away. But what good? He would only be arrested and lost. Yet he had dawdled his time, he had to run hard to catch the train in the end.

This time things went much more quickly. He was only two hours in the barracks. He was examined. He could tell they knew about him and disliked him. He was put in class C 3—unfit for military service, but conscripted for light non-military duties. There were no rejections now. Still, it was good enough. There were thousands of C men, men who *wanted* to have jobs as C men, so they were not very likely to fetch him up. He would only be a nuisance anyhow. That was clear all round.

Through the little window at the back of their ancient granite cottage, Harriet, peeping wistfully out to sea— poor Harriet, she was always frightened now—saw Richard coming across the fields, home, walking fast, and with that intent look about him that she half feared. She ran out in a sort of fear, then waited. She would wait.

He saw her face very bright with fear and joy at seeing him back: very beautiful in his eyes. The only real thing, perhaps, left in his world.

"Here you are! So early!" she cried. "I didn't expect you. The dinner isn't ready yet. Well?"

"C 3," he replied. "It's all right."

"I *knew* it would be," she cried, seizing his arm and hugging it to her. They went in to the cottage to finish cooking the evening meal. And immediately one of the farm girls came running up to see what it was.

"Oh, C 3—so you're all right, Mr Somers. Glad, I'm glad."

Harriet never forgot the straight, intent bee-line for home which he was making when she peeped out of that little window unaware.

So, another respite. They were not going to touch him. They knew he would be a firebrand in their army, a dangerous man to put with any group of men. They would leave him alone. C 3.

He had almost entirely left off writing now, and spent most of his days working on the farm. Again the neighbours were jealous.

"Buryan gets his labour cheap. He'd never have got his hay in but for Mr Somers," they said. And that was another reason for wishing to remove Richard Lovat. Work went like steam when he was on Trendrinnan farm, and he was too thick with the Buryans. Much too thick. And John Thomas Buryan rather bragged of Mr Somers at market, and how he, Richard Lovat, wasn't afraid of any of them, etc., etc.—that he wasn't going to serve anybody, etc.—and that nobody could make him—etc., etc.

But Richard drifted away this summer, on to the land, into the weather, into Cornwall. He worked out of doors all the time—he ceased to care inwardly—he began to drift away from himself. He was very thick with John Thomas, and nearly always at the farm. Harriet was a great deal alone. And he seemed to be drifting away, drifting back to the common people, becoming a working man, of the lower classes. It had its charm for Harriet, this aspect of him—careless, rather reckless, in old clothes and an old battered hat. He kept his sharp wits, but his *spirit* became careless, lost its concentration.

"I declare!" said John Thomas, as Somers appeared in the cornfield, "you look more like one of us every day." And he looked with a bright Cornish eye at Somers' careless, belted figure and old jacket. The speech struck Richard: it sounded half triumphant, half mocking. "He thinks I'm coming down in the world—it is half a rebuke," thought Somers to himself. But he was half pleased: and half he *was* rebuked.

Corn harvest lasted long, and was a happy time for them all. It went well, well. Also from London occasionally a young man came down and stayed at the inn in the church town, some young friend of Somers who hated the army and the Government and was generally discontented, and so fitfully came as an adherent to Richard Lovat. One of these was James Sharpe, a young Edinburgh man with a moderate income of his own, interested in music. Sharpe was hardly more than a lad—but he was the type of lowland Scotsman who is half an artist, not more, and so can never get on in the ordinary respectable life, rebels against it all the time, and yet can never get away from it or free himself from its dictates.

Sharpe had taken a house further along the coast, brought his piano down from London and sufficient furniture and a housekeeper, and insisted, like a morose bird, that he wanted to be alone. But he wasn't really morose, and he didn't want really to be alone. His old house, rather ramshackle, stood back a little way from the cliffs, where the moor came down savagely to the sea, past a deserted tin mine. It was lonely, wild, and in a savage way, poetic enough. Here Sharpe installed himself for the moment: to be alone with his music and his general discontent.

Of course he excited the wildest comments. He had window-curtains of different colours, so of course, *here* was plain signalling to the German submarines. Spies, the lot of them. When still another young man of the same set came and took a bungalow on the moors, West Cornwall decided that it was being delivered straight into German hands. Not that West Cornwall would really have minded that so terribly. No; it wasn't that it feared the Germans. It was that it hated the sight of these recalcitrant young men. And Somers the instigator, the arch-spy, the responsible little swine with his beard.

Somers, meanwhile, began to chuckle a bit to himself. After all he was getting the better of the military *canaille. Canaille! Canaglia! Schweinerei!* He loathed them in all the languages he could lay his tongue to.

So Somers and Harriet went to stay a week-end with Sharpe at Trevenna, as the house was called. Sharpe was a C 2 man, on perpetual tenterhooks. He had decided that if ever *he* were summoned to serve, he would just disappear. The Somers drove over, only three or four miles, on the Saturday afternoon, and the three wandered on the moor and down the cliff. No one was in sight. But how many pairs of eyes were watching, who knows? Sharpe lighting a cigarette for Harriet was an indication of untold immorality.

Evening came, the lamps were lit, and the incriminating curtains carefully drawn. The three sat before the fire in the long music room, and tried to be cosy and jolly. But there was something wrong with the mood. After dinner it was even worse. Harriet curled herself up on the sofa with a cigarette, Sharpe spread himself in profound melancholy in his big chair, Somers sat back, nearer the window. They talked in occasional snatches, in mockery of the enemy that surrounded them. Then Somers sang to himself, in an irritating way, one German folksong after another, not in a songful, but in a defiant way.

"Annchen von Tharau"—"Schatz, mein Schatz, reite nicht so weit von mir." "Zu Strasburg auf der Schanz, da fiel mein Unglück ein." This went on till Sharpe asked him to stop.

And in the silence, the tense and irritable silence that followed, came a loud bang. All got up in alarm, and followed Sharpe through the dining-room to the small entrance-room, where a dim light was burning. A lieutenant and three sordid men in the dark behind him, one with a lantern.

"Mr Sharpe?"—the authoritative and absolutely-in-the-right voice of the puppy lieutenant.

Sharpe took his pipe from his mouth and said laconically, "Yes."

"You've a light burning in your window facing the sea."

"I think not. There is only one window, and that's on the passage where I never go, upstairs."

"A light was showing from that window ten minutes ago."

"I don't think it can have been."

"It was." And the stern, puppy lieutenant turned to his followers, who clustered there in the dark.

"Yes, there was a light there ten minutes since," chimed the followers.

"I don't see how it's possible," persisted Sharpe.

"Oh, well—there is sufficient evidence that it was. What other persons have you in the house—" and this officer and gentleman stepped into the room, followed by his three Cornish weeds, one of whom had fallen into a ditch in his assiduous serving of his country, and was a sorry sight. Of course Harriet saw chiefly him, and had to laugh.

"There's Mrs Waugh, the housekeeper—but she's in bed."

The party now stood and eyed one another—the lieutenant with his three sorry braves on one hand, Sharpe, Somers, and Harriet in an old dress of soft silk on the other.

"Well, Mr Sharpe, the light was seen."

"I don't see how it was possible. We've none of us

been upstairs, and Mrs Waugh has been in bed for half an hour."

"Is there a curtain to the passage window?" put in Somers quietly. He had helped Sharpe in setting up house.

"I don't believe there is," said Sharpe. "I forgot all about it, as it wasn't in a room, and I never go to that side of the house. Even Mrs Waugh is supposed to go up the kitchen stairs, and so she doesn't have to pass it."

"She must have gone across with a candle as she went to bed," said Somers.

But the lieutenant didn't like being pushed into unimportance while these young men so quietly and naturally spoke together, excluding him as if he were an inferior: which they meant to do.

"You have an uncurtained window overlooking the sea, Mr Sharpe?" he said, in his military counter-jumper voice.

"You'll have to put a curtain to it to-morrow," said Somers to Sharpe.

"What is your name?" chimed the lieutenant.

"Somers—I wasn't speaking to you," said Richard coldly. And then to Sharpe, with a note of contempt: "That's what it is. Mrs Waugh must just have passed with a candle."

There was a silence. The wonderful watchers did not contradict.

"Yes, I suppose that's it," said Sharpe, fretfully.

"We'll put a curtain up to-morrow," said Somers.

The lieutenant would have liked to search the house.

He would have liked to destroy its privacy. He glanced down to the music room. But Harriet, so obviously a lady, even if a hateful one; and Somers with his pale look of derision; and Sharpe so impassive with his pipe; and the weedy watchers in the background, knowing just how it all was, and *almost* ready to take sides with the "gentleman" against the officer: they were too much for the lieutenant.

"Well, the light was there, Mr Sharpe. Distinctly visible from the sea," and he turned to his followers for confirmation.

"Oh, yes, a light plain enough," said the one who had fallen into a ditch, and wanted a bit of his own back.

"A candle!" said Sharpe, with his queer, musical note of derision and fretfulness. "A candle just passing—"

"You have an uncurtained window to the sea, and lights were showing. I shall have to report this to headquarters. Perhaps if you write and apologise to Major Caerlyon it may be passed over, if nothing of the like occurs again—"

So they departed, and the three went back to their room, fuming with rage and mockery. They mocked the appearance and voice of the lieutenant, the appearance of the weeds, and Harriet rejoiced over the one who had fallen into a ditch. This regardless of the fact that they knew now that *some* of the watchers were lying listening in the gorse bushes under the windows, and had been lying there all the evening.

"Shall you write and apologise?" said Somers.

"Apologise! no!" replied Sharpe, with peevish contempt.

Harriet and Somers went back home on the Monday. On the Tuesday appeared Sharpe, the police had been and left him a summons to appear at the market town, charged under the Defence of the Realm Act.

"I suppose you'll have to go," said Somers.

"Oh, I shall go," said he.

They waited for the day. In the afternoon Sharpe came with a white face and tears of rage and mortification in his eyes. The magistrate had told him he ought to be serving his country, and not causing mischief and skulking in an out-of-the-way corner. And had fined him twenty pounds.

"*I* shan't pay it," cried Sharpe.

"Your mother will," said Somers.

And so it was. What was the good of putting oneself in their power in *any* way, if it could be avoided?

So the lower fields were cleared of corn, and they started on the two big fields above on the moors. Sharpe cycled over to say a farmer had asked *him* to go and help at Westyr; and for once he had gone; but he felt spiteful to Somers for letting him in for this.

But Somers was very fond of the family at Buryan farm, and he loved working with John Thomas and the girls. John Thomas was a year or two older than Somers, and at this time his dearest friend. And so he loved working all day among the corn beyond the high-road, with the savage moors all round, and the hill with its pre-christian granite rocks rising like a great dark pyramid on the left, the sea in front. Sometimes a great airship hung over the sea, watching for submarines. The work stopped in the field, and the men watched. Then it went on again, and the wagon rocked slowly down the wild, granite road, rocked like a ship past Harriet's sunken cottage. But Somers stayed above all day, loading or picking, or resting, talking in the intervals with John Thomas, who loved a half-philosophical, mystical talking about the sun, and the moon, the mysterious powers of the moon at night, and the mysterious change in man with the change of season, and the mysterious effects of sex on a man. So they talked, lying in the bracken or on the heather as they waited for a wain. Or one of the girls came with dinner in a huge basket, and they ate all together, so happy with the moors and sky and touch of autumn. Somers loved these people. He loved the sensitiveness of their intelligence. They were not educated. But they had an endless curiosity about the world, and an endless interest in what was *right*.

"Now do you think it's right, Mr Somers?" The times that Somers heard that question, from the girls, from Arthur, from John Thomas. They spoke in the quick Cornish way, with the West Cornish accent. Sometimes it was:

"Now do'ee think it right?"

And with their black eyes they watched the ethical issue in his face. Queer it was. Right and wrong was not fixed for them as for the English. There was still a mystery for them in what was right and what was wrong. Only one thing was wrong—any sort of *physical* compulsion or hurt. That they were sure of. But as for the rest of behaviour—it was all a flux. They had none of the ethics of chivalry or of love.

Sometimes Harriet came also to tea: but not often. They loved her to come: and yet they were a little uneasy when she was there. Harriet was so definitely a lady. She liked them all. But it was a bit *noli me tangere*, with her. Somers was so *very* intimate with them. She couldn't be. And the girls said: "Mrs Somers don't mix in wi' the likes o' we like Mr Somers do." Yet they were always very pleased when Harriet came.

Poor Harriet spent many lonely days in the cottage. Richard was not interested in her now. He was only interested in John Thomas and the farm people, and he was growing more like a labourer every day. And the farm people didn't mind how long *she* was left alone, at night too, in that lonely little cottage, and with all the tension of fear upon her. Because she felt that it was *she* whom these authorities, these English, hated, even more than Somers. Because she made them feel she despised them. And as they were really rather despicable, they hated her at sight, her beauty, her reckless pride, her touch of derision. But Richard—even he neglected her and hated her. She was driven back on herself like a fury. And many a bitter fight they had, he and she.

The days grew shorter before the corn was all down from the moors. Sometimes Somers alone lay on the sheaves, waiting for the last wain to come to be loaded, while the others were down milking. And then the Cornish night would gradually come down upon the dark, shaggy moors, that were like the fur of some beast, and upon the pale-grey granite masses, so ancient and Druidical, suggesting blood-sacrifice. And as Somers sat there on the sheaves in the underdark, seeing the light swim above the sea, he felt he was over the border, in another world. Over the border, in that twilight, awesome world of the previous Celts. The spirit of the ancient, pre-Christian world, which lingers still in the truly Celtic places, he could feel it invade him in the savage dusk, making him savage too, and at the same time, strangely sensitive and subtle, understanding the mystery of blood-sacrifice: to sacrifice one's victim, and let the blood run to the fire, there beyond the gorse upon the old grey granite: and at the same time to understand most sensitively the dark flicker of animal life about him, even in a bat, even in the writhing of a maggot in a dead rabbit. Writhe then, Life, he seemed to say to the things—and he no longer saw its sickeningness.

RALPH DUNSTAN
(1857–1933)

I think we need a bit of uplifting after all Lawrence's storm and stress, so gather about and I'll teach you a song or two. I found them in *The Cornish Song Book*, a collection gathered by a musician, composer, writer and professor of music born at Carnon Downs. Ralph Dunstan began his studies at the new Wesleyan day school attached to the Truro chapel, going on to Westminster College and Cambridge University, where he gained his doctorate. On retirement, he moved back to Cornwall and began to collect shanties, carols and popular songs, as well as some original works and translations by the likes of J. C. Tregarthen, Henry Jenner and Dunstan himself.

Blow the Man Down

1

Oh blow the man down, bullies, blow the man down!
    Way ay!
Blow the man down! Oh blow him away, boys, to
    Liverpool town!
Gimme some time to blow the man down.

2

As I was a-walkin' down Killigrew Street, *Way ay*, etc.
A saucy young Bobby I chanc'd for to meet, *Gimme*, etc.

3

Sez he, "your'e a Smuggler, and that I can see; *Way
    ay*, etc.
So off to the Bodmin you go, Jack, wi' me; *Gimme*, etc.

4

"Your lugger is lyin' theer out by the Point; *Way ay*, etc.
You'll find I will soon put your noase out o' joint";
Gimme, etc.

5

Sez I, "you young loony, you think 'tis a lark, *Way*
     ay, etc.
For theer is my clipper, her name's 'Cutty Sark'."
Gimme, etc.

6

They gi' me three months in the "clink" o' the town,
     Way ay, etc.
For scruffin' that Bobby and blowin' him down!
Gimme, etc.

John Sturtridge and the Piskies

One *Picrous* night, from the "Rising Sun," Its sport
and dance and crowse,
John Sturtridge, prim'd and drunk with ale, Set out to
reach his house.
John's house was hard by holy Church In fam'd
Luxulyan town,
But now betwixt his home and him Lay drear
Tregarden Down.

So valiant John he trudg'd along His solitary road,
And port and starboard tack'd in turn, To fetch his
lov'd abode.
But when he reach'd a mighty stone, A boulder old
and grey,
He saw a sight which froze his blood And drove his
wits away.

It was the Piskies of the moor, A tiny roguish race,
Who nightly ride the farmers' steeds, And sheep and
oxen chase.
With cries of glee they follow'd John Along the beaten
track;
He hurried on at headlong speed, Not daring to look
back.

An hour or more he kept his pace, In sore amaze the
    while,
To find in all that moorland stretch No trace of gate
    or stile.
And great was John's surprise and fear, When,
    stopping his advance,
The Piskie circle hemm'd him round, With merry song
    and dance.

"Ho! Ho! and away," their leader said, His train quick
    answer gave,
"Ho! Ho! and away for the beach at Par, Beside the
    rolling wave."
Poor fluster'd John unwittingly Took up the mystic
    stave,
"Ho! Ho! and away for the beach at Par, Beside the
    rolling wave."

They whisk'd him through the air to Par, And there
    again beguil'd
Poor John with song and Piskie dance And revel weird
    and wild.
Then "Ho! and away," again they cried, The leader
    and his train,
"Ho! Ho! and away for Heligan House, The home of
    Squire Tremayne."

The cry was taken up by John, Too sorely dazed to
    think,

And briny beach and rolling wave All vanish'd in
  a wink.
And then to Heligan House they sped, And thro' the
  cellar door,
Where bins of wine and casks of beer Half hid the
  musty floor.

The beer and wine together mixed Ascended to his head,
And laid him low and made him think Himself at
  home in bed.
And when again the Piskie train Took up their
  former cry,
No answer came from sleepy John, So there they let
  him lie.

"Aw marcy me, where are I to? My awn good wife I
  miss;
'Tes dark and desmal, iss it ez, What wisht ould plaace
  is thes?
There's barrels oall around me, soas, I'm on the
  planshen flat,
Ef powder 'tes and they blaw up I'm oall to pieces
  skat!"

"You rascal you, what do you here, You beast without
  a tail?
You guzzling drunken thief, I'll have You lock'd up
  safe in jail."
John pleaded hard for liberty, But all without avail,

Was taken, tried, condemn'd to die, And lock'd up in
    the jail.

But when they took him out to hang, Right 'neath the
    gallows-tree,
A "little lady" there did stand, In shrill sweet voice
    sang she;
"Ho, Ho! and away, away to France," "Away to
    France," said he,
And thro' the air away they went To join the
    Piskies free.

A Cornish Smuggler's Song

Of Prussia Cove, where I was born,
  A song I here begin;
My father is a smuggler bold,
  And well do he "knaw tin;"
To "land a cargo of the goods"
  He never thought a sin.
    And 'tis my delight on a moonless night
To run a cargo in.

John Carter is my father's name,
  The King of all his kin;
He is an "honest man," and keeps
  His word thro' thick and thin;
For mounted men and cutlass'd guard
  He doesn't care a pin.
    And 'tis my delight on a moonless night
To run a cargo in.

Our lugger is the Rose and Crown,
  We bought her at Penryn;
A double-bottom, too, has she,
  As snug as any bin.
To see the tubs she brings from France
  Would make a dunkey grin!

And 'tis my delight on a moonless night
To run a cargo in.

No mark of keg or sinking-stone
  Is ever seen within;
Across the Channel, rough or smooth,
  So sweetly does she spin.
What joy my boys to "land the goods,"
  Nor lose a kilderkin!
    And 'tis my delight on a moonless night
To run a cargo in.

We've friends galore along the shore:
  There's dear old Squire Prynne,
And ev'ry farmer near and far,
  And Mathey at the inn;
And passun Vigurs doant despise
  A case of Hollands gin!
    And 'tis my delight on a moonless night
To run a cargo in.

Poor speed to all Preventive spies
  From Tresco Sands to Lyn;
They'd saw a poor man's boat in dree,
  And joy to do him in!
Why should they take the bread away
  We work so hard to win?
    And 'tis my delight on a moonless night
To run a cargo in.

The Boats of Sennen

The corn is in the shock,
And the fish are on the rock,
And the merry boats go dancing out of Whitesand Bay,
   I hear the huer's cry,
   And I see the dappled sky,
And it minds of me of the days that are long gone
      away.

The corn was in the shock,
And the fish were on the rock,
And the sea was all alive from the Wolf to Castle Treen,
   But the fog came down by night,
   And it hid the Longships light,
And the men that went a fishing never, never, more
      were seen.

The corn was in the shock,
And the fish were on the rock,
When the boats went out from Sennen with the
      pilchard seine;
   But the morning broke so fair,
   And not a boat was there,
And the lad I lov'd was with them and he came not
      back again.

The corn is in the shock,
And the fish are on the rock,
And the golden sun is gleaming on the Islands of the
West:
I hear the huer's cry,
And I see the dappled sky,
But my heart is dead with sorrow for the lad I love the
best.

The Mermaid

One Friday morning we set sail,
And when not far from land,
We all espied a fairy merry maid
With a comb and a glass in her hand, her hand, her
    hand,
With a comb and a glass in her hand.

While the raging seas did roar,
And the stormy winds did blow,
And we jolly sailor boys were sitting up aloft,
And the land lubbers lying down below, below, below,
And the land lubbers lying down below.

Then up starts the captain of our gallant ship,
And a brave young man was he;
"I've a wife and a daughter in fair Helston town,
But I fear they'll be weeping for me, for me, for me,
But I fear they'll be weeping for me."

Then up starts the mate of our gallant ship,
And a bold young man was he;
"Oh, I have a wife in fair Padstow town,
But I fear she a widow will be, will be, will be,
But I fear she a widow will be."

Then up starts the cook of our gallant ship,
And a fine young man was he;
"Oh, I have a sweetheart in fair Lanson town,
But I fear she'll be weeping for me, for me, for me,
But I fear she'll be weeping for me."

And then up spoke the little cabin boy,
And a pretty little boy was he;
"Oh, I am more sorry for my daddy and my mammy,
Who will both be a-weeping for me, for me, for me,
Who will both be a-weeping for me."

Then three times round went our gallant ship,
And three times round went she;
For the want of a long-boat we all went down—
And she sank to the bottom of the sea, the sea,
    the sea,
And she sank to the bottom of the sea.

Chorus (repeat *ad lib*)

WILLIAM BOTTRELL
(1816–1881)

Talking of mermaids, we can't visit Zennor without mentioning her, can we? The earliest written version of this famous tale is told by the 'Old Celt' William Bottrell in his *Traditions and Hearthside Stories of West Cornwall*. The mermaid's chair of the story remains in the south transept of the church of St Senara in Zennor to this day.

'The Mermaid of Zennor'

Zennor folks tell the following story, which, according to them, accounts for a singular carving on a bench-end in their Church.

Hundreds of years ago a very beautiful and richly attired lady attended service in Zennor Church occasionally—now and then she went to Morvah also;—her visits were by no means regular,—often long intervals would elapse between them.

Yet whenever she came the people were enchanted with her good looks and sweet singing. Although Zennor folks were remarkable for their fine psalmody, she excelled them all; and they wondered how, after the scores of years that they had seen her, she continued to look so young and fair. No one knew whence she came nor whither she went; yet many watched her as far as they could see from Tregarthen Hill.

She took some notice of a fine young man, called Mathey Trewella, who was the best singer in the parish. He once followed her, but he never returned; after that she was never more seen in Zennor Church, and it might not have been known to this day who or what she was but for the merest accident.

One Sunday morning a vessel cast anchor about a mile from Pendower Cove; soon after a mermaid came close alongside and hailed the ship. Rising out of the water as far as her waist, with her yellow hair floating around her, she told the captain that she was returning from church, and requested him to trip his anchor just for a minute, as the fluke of it rested on the door of her dwelling, and she was anxious to get in to her children.

Others say that while she was out on the ocean a-fishing of a Sunday morning, the anchor was dropped on the trap-door which gave access to her submarine abode. Finding, on her return, how she was hindered from opening her door, she begged the captain to have the anchor raised that she might enter her dwelling to dress her children and be ready in time for church.

However it may be, her polite request had a magical effect upon the sailors, for they immediately "worked with a will," hove anchor and set sail, not wishing to remain a moment longer than they could help near her habitation. Sea-faring men, who understood most about mermaids, regarded their appearance as a token that bad luck was near at hand. It was believed they could take such shapes as suited their purpose, and that they had often allured men to live with them.

When Zennor folks learnt that a mermaid dwelt near Pendower, and what she had told the captain, they concluded it was this sea-lady who had visited their church, and enticed Trewella to her abode. To commemorate these somewhat unusual events they had the figure she bore—when in her ocean-home—carved in holy-oak, which may still be seen.

A Riddle for the Windy Road to St Ives

As I was going to St Ives,
I met a man with seven wives,
Every wife had seven sacks,
Every sack had seven cats,
Every cat had seven kits:
Kits, cats, sacks, and wives,
How many were there going to St Ives?

'THE FAIRY WIDOWER'
collected by Robert Hunt

Yes, yes, there are artists here. Lots of artists and writers and a good gallery or two. But before even they came to this area – the moors and the coast around Zennor, Towednack and St Ives – there were little folk living here.

There are lots of little folk in Cornwall. Some you can hear at work in the mines, while others take your horse in the night and ride until it's exhausted. Some steal children and lure young people away to the fairy realm; others draw you into the marshes at night to drown. Others still are more domestic, helping around the house and farm. (Remember, they prefer to help at tidy homes!) Fewer fairies are seen today, but keep your eyes peeled; there have been recent reports around St Austell Bay, Looe, Carbis Bay and Porthtowan, among other places. The following story begins in Towednack.

'The Fairy Widower'

Not many years since a very pretty girl called Jenny Permuen lived in Towednack. She was of poor parents, and lived in service. There was a good deal of romance, or what the old people called nonsense, in Jenny. She was always smartly dressed, and she would arrange wildflowers very gracefully in her hair. As a consequence, Jenny attracted much of the attention of the young men, and again, as a consequence, a great deal of envy from the young women. Jenny was, no doubt, vain; and her vanity, which most vain persons will say is not usual, was accompanied by a considerable amount of weakness on any point connected with her person. Jenny loved flattery, and being a poor, uneducated girl, she had not the genius necessary to disguise her frailty. When any man told her she was lovely, she quite admitted the truth of the assertion by her pleased looks. When any woman told her not to be such a fool as to believe such nonsense, her lips, and eyes too, seemed to say you are only jealous of me, and if there was a pool of water near, nature's mirror was speedily consulted to prove to herself that she was really the best-looking girl in the parish. Well, one day Jenny, who had been for some time out of a situation, was sent by her mother down to the lower parishes to "look for a place." Jenny went on merrily enough until she came to the four cross roads on the Lady Downs, when she discovered that she knew not which road to take. She looked first one way and then another, and she felt fairly puzzled, so she sat down on a boulder of granite, and began, in pure want of thought, to break off the beautiful fronds of ferns which grew abundantly around the spot she had chosen. It is hard to say what her intentions were, whether to go on, to return, or to remain where she was, so utterly indifferent did Jenny appear. Some say she was entirely lost in wild dreams of self-glorification. However, she had not sat long on this granite stone, when hearing a voice near her, she turned round and saw a young man.

"Well, young woman," says he, "and what are you after?"

"I am after a place, sir," says she.

"And what kind of a place do you want, my pretty young woman?" says he, with the most winning smile in the world.

"I am not particular, sir," says Jenny; "I can make myself generally useful."

"Indeed," says the stranger; "do you think you could look after a widower with one little boy?"

"I am very fond of children," says Jenny.

"Well, then," says the widower, "I wish to hire for a year and a day a young woman of your age, to take charge of my little boy."

"And where do you live?" inquired Jenny.

"Not far from here," said the man; "will you go with me and see?"

"An it please you to show me," said Jenny.

"But first, Jenny Permuen,"—Jenny stared when she

found the stranger knew her name. He was evidently an entire stranger in the parish, and how could he have learnt her name, she thought. So she looked at him somewhat astonished. "Oh! I see, you suppose I didn't know you; but do you think a young widower could pass through Towednack and not be struck with such a pretty girl? Beside," he said, "I watched you one day dressing your hair in one of my ponds, and stealing some of my sweet-scented violets to put in those lovely tresses. Now, Jenny Permuen, will you take the place?"

"For a year and a day?" asked Jenny.

"Yes, and if we are pleased with each other then, we can renew the engagement."

"Wages," said Jenny.

The widower rattled the gold in his breeches-pocket.

"Wages! well, whatever you like to ask," said the man.

Jenny was charmed; all sorts of visions rose before her eyes, and without hesitation she said—

"Well, I'll take the place, sir; when must I come?"

"I require you now—my little boy is very unhappy, and I think you can make him happy again. You'll come at once?"

"But mother—"

"Never mind mother, I'll send word to her."

"But my clothes—"

"The clothes you have will be all you require, and I'll put you in a much gayer livery soon."

"Well, then," says Jenny, "'tis a bargain."

"Not yet," says the man; "I've got a way of my own, and you must swear my oath."

Jenny looked frightened.

"You need not be alarmed," said the man, very kindly; "I only wish you to kiss that fern-leaf which you have in your hand, and say, 'For a year and a day I promise to stay.'"

"Is that all?" said Jenny; so she kissed the fern-leaf and said—

> "For a year and a day
> I promise to stay."

Without another word he walked forward on the road leading eastward. Jenny followed him—she thought it strange that her new master never opened his lips to her all the way, and she grew very tired with walking. Still onward and onward he went, and Jenny was sadly weary and her feet dreadfully sore. At last poor Jenny began to cry. He heard her sob and looked round.

"Tired are you, poor girl? Sit down—sit down," says the man, and he took her by the hand and led her to a mossy bank. His kindness completely overcame her, and she burst into a flood of tears. He allowed her to cry for a few minutes, then taking a bunch of leaves from the bottom of the bank, he said, "Now I must dry your eyes, Jenny."

He passed the bunch of leaves rapidly first over one and then over the other eye.

The tears were gone. Her weariness had departed. She felt herself moving, yet she did not know that she had moved from the bank. The ground appeared to open, and they were passing very rapidly under the earth. At last there was a pause.

"Here we are, Jenny," said he, "there is yet a tear of sorrow on your eyelids, and no human tears can enter our homes, let me wipe them away." Again Jenny's eyes were brushed with the small leaves as before, and, lo! before her was such a country as she had never seen previously. Hill and valley were covered with flowers, strangely varied in colour, but combining into a most harmonious whole; so that the region appeared sown with gems which glittered in a light as brilliant as that of the summer sun, yet as mild as the moonlight. There were rivers clearer than any water she had ever seen on the granite hills, and waterfalls and fountains; while everywhere ladies and gentlemen dressed in green and gold were walking, or sporting, or reposing on banks of flowers, singing songs or telling stories. Oh! it was a beautiful world.

"Here we are at home," said Jenny's master; and strangely enough he too was changed; he was the most beautiful little man she had ever seen, and he wore a green silken coat covered with ornaments of gold. "Now," said he again, "I must introduce you to your little charge." He led Jenny into a noble mansion in which all the furniture was of pearl and ivory, inlaid with gold and silver, and studded with emeralds. After passing through many rooms, they came at length to one which was hung all over with lace, as fine as the finest cobweb, most beautifully worked with flowers; and, in the middle of this room was a little cot made out of some beautiful sea-shell, which reflected so many colours that Jenny could scarcely bear to look at it. She was led to the side of this, and she saw, as she said, "One of God's sweetest angels sleeping there." The little boy was so beautiful that she was ravished with delight.

"This is your charge," said the father; "I am the king in this land, and I have my own reasons for wishing my boy to know something of human nature. Now you have nothing to do but to wash and dress the boy when he wakes, to take him to walk in the garden, and to put him to bed when he is weary."

Jenny entered on her duties, and gave, and continued to give, satisfaction. She loved the darling little boy, and he appeared to love her, and the time passed away with astonishing rapidity.

Somehow or other she had never thought of her mother. She had never thought of her home at all. She was happy and in luxury, and never reckoned the passing of time.

Howsoever happiness my blind us to the fact, the hours and days move onward. The period for which Jenny had bound herself was gone, and one morning she awoke and all was changed. She was sleeping in her own bed in her mother's cottage. Everything was strange to her, and she appeared strange to everybody. Numerous old gossips were called in to see Jenny, and to all Jenny told her strange tale alike. One day, old Mary Calineck of Zennor came, and she heard, as all the others had done, the story of the widower, and the baby, and the beautiful country. Some of the old crones who were there at the time said the girl was "gone clean daft." Mary looked very wise—"Crook your arm, Jenny," said she.

Jenny sat up in the bed and bent her arm, resting her hand on her hip.

"Now say, I hope my arm may never come uncrooked if I have told ye a word of a lie."

"I hope my arm may never come uncrooked if I have told ye a word of a lie," repeated Jenny.

"Uncrook your arm," said Mary.

Jenny stretched out her arm.

"It is truth the girl is telling," said Mary; "and she has been carried by the Small People to some of their countries under the hills."

"Will the girl ever come right in her mind?" asked her mother.

"All in good time," said Mary; "and if she will but be honest, I have no doubt but her master will take care that she never wants."

Howbeit, Jenny did not get on very well in the world. She married and was discontented and far from happy. Some said she always pined after the fairy widower. Others said they were sure she had misbehaved herself, or she would have brought back lots of gold. If Jenny had not dreamt all this, while she was sitting picking ferns on the granite boulder, she had certainly had a very strange adventure.

EDITH ELLIS
(1861–1916)

Though born up country, Edith Ellis settled in a cottage in Carbis Bay and remained there most of her adult life, writing books, essays and lectures on marriage reform and experimentation, social and economic independence for women, sexual reform and eugenics, as well as stories about her neighbours.

Ironically, given her activism for independence within marriage, Edith Ellis's name is usually chained to that of her husband, the sexologist Havelock Ellis, to the extent that even on the title pages of her books she is 'Mrs Havelock Ellis'. Their marriage was of the experimental type she advocated, with Edith not being romantically attracted to men and their openness allowing her to develop lesbian relationships at the same time.

The following little tale is from *My Cornish Neighbours*. Most of the stories are lightly humorous, like the dialect tales popular in almanacks and newspapers, but some have a darker edge. They tend to be domestic scenes; a neighbour coming for a chat and a gossip about the new policeman or a lost son while knitting or sitting around the fire.

'Lightning'

"My head's like needles and pins," said Tobias Penberthy irritably. "I feel as if I've been flayed by a yard broom made wi' wire." He looked at Bob Olds and shook his head. Olds was a thickset man, who sat comfortably in the corner of his fireplace smoking a little clay pipe.

"It was some dirty weather last night, sure enough," Olds replied stolidly, "but I rather likes the feelin' of bein' tucked in comfortable while the elements is roarin' outside. It ain't often as there's thunder, lightning, and hail all to onc'st."

"Thanks be!" said Tobias.

"We must take it as it comes," said a gentle-voiced woman who was knitting in the corner, and who raised her head now and again to catch what her husband and his friend were saying.

"We ain't no choice," said Bob.

"Lightnin's a fearsome thing," said Tobias.

"It's like fireworks to some," said Bob.

"It's like death to others," said Bob's wife.

"It was to the cat," said her husband, yawning.

"I've never seen no such things," he went on.

"The poor beast shook for hours wi' its tongue out, and panted as if it had run miles, its eyes dartin' out of its head like as if it was mad. The chintzycat, now, might have been born and reared i' claps o' thunder, the way she purred and lapped her milk."

"It's different dispositions," said Tobias.

"It's pluck," said Bob.

His wife's knitting needles flicked in the firelight as she said gently:

"Perhaps it's a voice to some, and nothin' but a noise to others."

Bob laughed. Tobias looked across at his friend's wife, and the two men puffed hard at their pipes. Bob at last got up, tapped on the stove to knock the ashes out of his pipe, and then stretched himself and clasped his big hands over his head.

"You can never reckon," he said, looking at his wife Grace, "what way women is going to take anything up." Then, jerking his thumb towards her, he added: "I sometimes think she's worse nor a play-actor for fancies."

The woman was counting stitches in the heel of her sock, and her lips moved. Tobias watched her for a few minutes and then glanced at Bob.

"She do keep a cozie home for thee, Bob, in spite of fancies," said Tobias, and he sighed as he spoke.

"I'd beat a woman as was a slut or a snap-tongue," said Bob.

Grace glanced at her husband, and Tobias sighed again.

"Thee may well sigh," said Bob roughly. "Thee's never had no real go and pluck in thee since thy last dance at the Cat and Whistle. It was most the end of thee. Thy wife 'ave triumphed over thee now till thee do end or she do end i' the cemetery."

Tobias frowned as he said:

"You'm right, Bob, and a sudden storm like this 'ere do sometimes give me hope, for you never know when your turn may come. I knew a man once as took lightning as a sort o' friend, but that was 'cause it saved his life. I should reckon it mine if—"

Grace looked up suddenly and held her finger on one stitch so as not to forget her counting, and her face was pale as she spoke.

"A friend?" she said.

"Iss!" said Tobias.

"Tell about him," said Bob, and he stretched out his legs towards the blaze. The woman folded her thin hands over the sock she had laid in her lap.

"He were a man I knew quite well when I was a boy," Tobias began. "One night, out on the cliffs, he were overtaken wi' a storm like we had last night. It were pitch black, like ink, and the thunder and lightning seemed to fight one another to see which could do the worst. And then, sudden like, the lightning stopped, and the thunder too, and the hail came down like pebbles, so, though the man knew every inch of the cliff road, as he thought, he could not find the path before him. He got scared, and turned to the left, 'oping it would lead him out by the lane near his house." Tobias cleared his throat, and coughed as he went on: "It allus gives me the crawls when I think upon what that chap went through that night, and I often start at the thoughts of it when I wake sudden like." Grace's eyes were fixed on the speaker's face, and Bob was cramming his pipe with fresh tobacco.

"Why! What happened?" asked his wife.

Tobias turned towards her as he answered:

"He had his foot over the cliff as he turned to the left, and a g'eat flash o' lightning come that second, and he saw that it were just i' time. He told me he stood like that, wi' his foot in the air, for long enough, for all the power had gone out of his limbs. Flash after flash came, and still he could not move. He said he felt bound to stay there and watch, same as if he was bewitched."

"Why! What did he see?" asked Grace, in a low voice.

"Death in 'Hell's Mouth,'" said Tobias slowly.

"He were just over it, and in less time than I take to tell it he would have been a dead man but for that flash of lightning."

"Enough to make a minister of him," said Bob roughly.

The woman said nothing, but folded her hands together over her knitting and looked into the fire. Tobias glanced at her as if expecting her to speak, but as she did not he went on. "No, it never took him a bit like that. He never seemed to think it was the hand of the Lord at all, but somethin' life-like in the lightning itself. Chaps used to tease him often about it, for just as some go crazy wi' terror when a storm's brewin', he looked then for all the world as a man does when he's goin' to see his sweetheart."

The woman began knitting again as she said:

"I never heard of no such thing before."

"It's yarns, seems to me," said Bob.

"No, it ain't," said Tobias quietly. "It's gospel truth. Over everythin' else the man was as hard as nails, and had no soft feelin's for women nor childer, nor even cats and such like, but the lightning allus made a new man of him; he'd sit alone with it for hours, never go nigh no one when a storm was on, and was for days after it was over a quiet, good-natured chap, ready to do a turn for anybody. Nobody could make it up, and no more can I," ended Tobias thoughtfully.

"Worse nor a woman's fancy, that," said Bob.

"I can't abide whims and unbeknowns ideas o' that kind; they allus make me sick."

"Perhaps it was unavoidable in him," said Grace.

"What's strong in the heart must out some way."

Bob scratched his head with the stem of his pipe, which he rubbed between his finger and thumb, and began smoking again as he said:

"Grace is the sort as could get a whimey notion like that over lightning, and there'd be no puttin' it out of her head if she did," he said, as he jerked his thumb towards her.

There was a pause.

"Do the lightning fuss you at all, Mrs Olds?" asked Tobias gently.

The woman smiled as she answered:

"No, it do never make much difference to me one way nor another. I allus take what comes just as it comes, but," and she looked nervously towards her husband, "of course, I do allus feel it can cause sudden death at times, and though I know it is a quick and easy way of dyin'," she added softly, "still, I should not like to be unprepared, and so I allus puts clean pillow-slips on the bed when a storm comes for fear we should be took sudden in the night, for I should like to be found clean and tidy, however quick my end was."

Bob gazed into the fire and smoked harder than ever, and Tobias stopped smoking and looked at the woman as she ceased.

JOHN HARRIS
(1820–1884)

Heading back east, we need to go inland a minute. We'll pause at Camborne for a poem, shall we? These inland towns are too often overlooked, yet Camborne was one of the most important centres for tin and copper mining in the world, and one of its greatest mines was Dolcoath, where John Harris worked.

Harris worked here from the age of twelve and spent more than two decades underground, which was normal enough, but what was unusual was he left the mines with his life and his health and he learned to read and write.

Harris's enthusiasm for books was encouraged by teachers and mine captains alike and in those early days he borrowed books from their personal libraries, writing in snatched moments either on the three-mile journey to Dolcoath or in the evenings after work by the light of the fire, using the bellows as a writing desk and the juice of blackberries when ink was scarce.

The Mine

A travelling youth hastes down the village lane
All fever'd with excitement. By the well
He meets a matron with her jar and jug;
And as she dips them in the crystal fount,
He asks her, pointing with his hazel staff,
"Who lives across the coppice in yon house
They say was haunted many years ago?
Though for my part I can't believe a ghost
Would quit the bowers of angels for this place,
To dwell with rats and cobwebs. Fie on it!
I've heard my father say how oft strange lights
Would flare along the damp rooms windowless,
And solemn dirges at still midnight rose,
And songs were heard when nought but winds were
    there:
And so the people said the manor-house
Was haunted with the strangest, wildest things.
Old women's fancies! why, I've walked o'er graves,
And fields of dead, and mounds of rotting bones,
When stars were blinking in the deeps of heaven;

And I have often pray'd to see a ghost,
If ghosts are palpable to mortal ken;
But not a phantom raised his shadowy arm.
When last I saw this dwelling, years ago,

'T was weeping in its ruins: now it looks
The abode of plenty, where red faces meet.
Pray, can you tell me who the owner is?"
And when she told him that its present lord
Was once the tinner living on the moor,
Who ventured till the mice forsook his shelf
And leanness seized upon him, he exclaim'd,
"O change of changes! 'tis my father's home."

Full soon he cross'd the greenwood, praising much
The grand old trees that seem'd to welcome him
To linger in their cloisters. Then he stood
Within the ivy archway, lost in thought.
And now his hands are playing with the vine
About the porch; and now he knocks the door,
And soon is weeping in his mother's arms.
Then father comes, but how unlike the man
He left half-starved within his frigid hut,
Still struggling, striving, hoping against hope!
A portly person now with manly air,
And much that's pleasant peering from his eye.
Then tales were told and loving questions ask'd,
And lengthy queries answer'd, till the moon
Slid into midnight with her suite of stars,
And prayer uprose among the listening trees.
Then he lay down to dream of other days,
And one bright vision flitted though his brain.

Next morn his father took him on a hill
Within his own estate, where cattle grazed

And finest sheep were feeding. Far below,
Upon the very spot the dragon roll'd
Where the bold honest tinner lost and won,
A mine spread out its vast machinery.
Here engines, with their huts and smoky stacks,
Cranks, wheels, and rods, boilers and hissing steam,
Press'd up the water from the depths below.
Here fire-whims ran till almost out of breath,
And chains cried sharply, strain'd with fiery force.
Here blacksmiths hammer'd by the sooty forge,
And there a crusher crash'd the copper ore.
Here girls were cobbing under roofs of straw,
And there were giggers at the oaken hutch.
Here a man-engine glided up and down,
A blessing and a boon to mining men:
And near the spot where, many years before,
Turn'd round and round the rude old water-wheel,
A huge fire-stamps was working evermore,
And slimy boys were swarming at the trunks.
The noisy lander by the trap-door bawl'd
With pincers in his hand; and troops of maids
With heavy hammers brake the mineral stones.
The cart-man cried, and shook his broken whip;
And on the steps of the account-house stood
The active agent, with his eye on all.

Below were caverns grim with greedy gloom,
And levels drunk with darkness; chambers huge
Where Fear sat silent, and the mineral-sprite
For ever chanted his bewitching song;

Shafts deep and dreadful, looking darkest things
And seeming almost running down to doom;
Rock under foot, rock standing on each side;
Rock cold and gloomy, frowning overhead;
Before, behind, at every angle, rock.
Here blazed a vein of precious copper ore,
Where lean men labour'd with a zeal for fame,
With face and hands and vesture black as night,
And down their sides the perspiration ran
In steaming eddies, sickening to behold.
But they complain'd not, digging day and night,
And morn and eve, with lays upon their lips.
Here yawn'd a tin-cell like a cliff of crags,
And Danger lurk'd among the groaning rocks,
And ofttimes moan'd in darkness. All the air
Was black with sulphur, burning up the blood.
A nameless mystery seem'd to fill the void,
And wings all pitchy flapp'd among the flints,
And eyes that saw not sparkled mid the spars.
Yet here men work'd, on stages hung in ropes,
With drills and hammers blasting the rude earth,
Which fell with such a crash that he who heard
Cried, "Jesu, save the miner!" Here were ends
Cut through hard marble by the miners' skill,
And winzes, stopes, and rises: pitches here,
Where work'd the heroic, princely tributer,
This month for nothing, next for fifty pounds.
Here lodes ran wide, and there so very small
That scarce a pick-point could be press'd between;
Here making walls as smooth as polish'd steel,

And there as craggy as a rended hill:
And out of sparry vagues the water oozed,
Staining the rock with mineral, so that oft
It led the labourer to a house of gems.
Across the mine a hollow cross-course ran
From north to south, an omen of much good;
And tin lay heap'd on stulls and level-plots;
And in each nook a tallow taper flared,
Where pale men wasted with exhaustion huge.
Here holes exploded, and there mallets rang,
And rocks fell crashing, lifting the stiff hair
From time-worn brows, and noisy buckets roar'd
In echoing shafts; and through this gulf of gloom
A hollow murmur rush'd for evermore.

And then the father and his wondering boy
Cross'd the rude moors, conversing as they went,
When the youth learnt his father sold the mine
For thousands upon thousands, keeping still
Large shares of profit for himself and son.
And as they linger'd by a broken stile,
Watching a flock of rooks wheel o'er the wood,
And breathing odours from the banks of flowers,
A group of mining men came down the lane,
With footsteps fleet, and very sad of face,
Bearing a burden on some unplaned boards
Nail'd carelessly together. 'T was a youth
Who left his mother on the lonely wild
At dead of night, to dig within the mine.
He was her only son; the rest were drown'd,

And so this boy became her sole support.
And rumour ran he courted a fair maid,
Whose fame was like a rose-bud, and next moon
They would be married in the village church.
But Providence had order'd otherwise;
For while he labour'd, tamping up a hole
In a hard cross-cut, ninety fathoms down,
It crash'd around him, killing him outright;
And so his mangled form, lash'd to a spar,
Was drawn up through the shaft, and borne along
By his sad comrades to his mother's hut;
And fleetly pass'd they over hill and dale,
Till lost among the rising mists of morn.

WINSTON GRAHAM
(1908–2003)

Winston Graham's Poldark saga is set in a semi-fictional Cornwall around the Perranporth area, where Graham himself lived for many years. The following extract is from the first book in the series, *Ross Poldark*. Ross has recently married his young servant Demelza and pilchards have been spotted off Sawle, so the couple head out to watch as the fishermen bring in the catch.

from Ross Poldark

Pilchards had come late to the coast that year. The delay had caused anxiety, for not only did the livelihood of many people depend on the arrival of the fish but virtually in these times their existence. In the Scillies and the extreme south the trade was already in full swing, and there were always wiseacres and pessimists who were ready to predict that the shoals would miss the northern shores of the county this year and go across to Ireland instead.

A sigh of relief greeted the news that a catch had been made at St Ives, but the first shoal was not sighted off Sawle until the afternoon of the sixth of August.

A huer, watching from the cliff, as he had been watching for weeks, spotted the familiar dark red tinge far out to sea, and the cry he let out through his old tin trumpet inspirited the village. The seining boats instantly put out, seven men to each of the leading boats, four to the follower.

Towards evening it was known that both teams had made catches much above the average, and the news spread with great speed. Men working on the harvest at once downed tools and hurried to the village, followed by every free person from Grambler and many of the miners as they came off core.

Jud had been into Grambler that afternoon and

came back with the news to Demelza, who told Ross over their evening meal.

'I'm that glad,' she said. 'All Sawle've been wearing faces down to their chins. Twill be a rare relief; and I hear it is a handsome catch.'

Ross's eyes followed her as she rose from the table and went to trim the wicks of the candles before they were lighted. He had been at the mine all day and had enjoyed his supper in the shadowy parlour with the evening stealing into and about the room. There was no real difference between now and that evening two months ago when he had come home defeated and it had all begun. Jim Carter was still in prison. There was no real change in the futility of his own life and efforts.

'Demelza,' he said.

'Um?'

'It is low tide at eleven,' he said. 'And the moon's up. What if we rowed round to Sawle and watched them putting down the tuck net.'

'Ross, that would be lovely!'

'Shall we take Jud to help row us?' This to tease.

'No, no, let us go, just the two of us! Let us go alone. You and I, Ross.' She was almost dancing before his chair. 'I will row. I am as strong as Jud any day. We'll go an' watch, just the two of us alone.'

He laughed. 'You'd think it was a ball I'd invited you to. D'you think I can't row you that far myself?'

'When shall we start?'

'In an hour.'

'Good, good, good. I'll make ready something to

eat – an' brandy in a flask, lest it be cold sitting, an' – an' a rug for me, and a basket for some fish.' She fairly ran from the room.

They set off for Nampara Cove shortly after nine. It was a warm still evening with the three-quarter moon already high. In Nampara Cove they dragged their small boat from the cave where it was kept, across the pale firm sand to the sea's edge. Demelza got in and Ross pushed the boat through the fringe of whispering surf and jumped in as it floated.

The sea was very calm tonight and the light craft was quite steady as he pulled towards the open sea. Demelza sat in the stern and watched Ross and looked about her and dipped a hand over the gunnel to feel the water trickling between her fingers. She was wearing a scarlet kerchief about her hair and a warm skin coat which had belonged to Ross as a boy and now just fitted her.

They skirted the high bleak cliffs between Nampara Cove and Sawle Bay, and the jutting rocks stood in sharp silhouette against the moonlit sky. The water sucked and slithered about the base of the cliffs. They passed two inlets which were inaccessible except by boat at any tide, being surrounded by steep cliffs. All this was as familiar to Ross as the shape of his own hand, but Demelza had never seen it. She had only once been out in a boat before. They passed the Queen Rock, where a number of good ships had come to grief, and then rounded a promontory into Sawle Bay and came on the first fishers.

They had let down the seine net – a fine strong mesh

of great length, with corks on the upper side and lead on the lower – some distance past the promontory and about half a mile from the shore. With this great net the seiners had enclosed about two acres of water and, they hoped, many fish. There was always the possibility, of course, that they had been wrongly directed by the man on the cliffs who alone could see the movement of the shoal, or that some flaw on the sea bed should have prevented the net from falling cleanly and so allowed the fish to slip away. But short of such accidents there was every hope of a good catch. And although in calm weather it might be possible to keep the net in position by means of grapnels for ten days or a fortnight, no one had the least intention of relying on good weather a minute longer than they had to.

And tonight there was a moon.

As low tide approached the boat known as the follower and carrying the tuck net was rowed cautiously into the enclosed area marked by the bobbing corks supporting the great stop seine. The boat was rowed round within the area while the tuck net was lowered and secured at various points. This done, they began to haul in the tuck net again.

It was at this crucial stage that Ross and Demelza came closely on the scene. They were not the only spectators. Every boat that would float and every human being that could sit in one had come out from Sawle to watch. And those who had no craft or were too infirm stood on the shelving beach and shouted advice or encouragement. There were lights and lanterns in the cottages of Sawle and all along the shingle bar and moving up and down on the blue-white waters of the cove. The moon lit up the scene with an unreal twilight.

Sea gulls flapped and screamed low overhead. No one took much notice of the new arrivals. One or two called friendly greetings. The arrival of Ross on the scene did not embarrass them as the arrival of others of the gentry might have done.

He rowed his boat close to where the master seiner was standing in his craft giving brief orders to the men who were within the circle hauling in the net. As it became clear that the net was heavy a short silence fell. In a moment or two it would be known whether the catch was a fine or a poor one, whether they had trapped a good part of the shoal or some part with fish too small for salting and export, whether by some mischance they might have caught a shoal of sprats instead, as had happened a couple of years ago. On the result of the next few minutes the prosperity of half the village hung.

The only sound now was the bobble and swish of water against fifty keels and the deep 'Yoy . . . ho! Hoy . . . ho!' chorus of the men straining to haul in the net.

Up and up came the net. The master seiner had forgotten his words of advice and stood there biting his fingers and watching the waters within the tuck net for the first sign of life.

It was not long in coming. First one of the spectators said something, then another exclaimed. Then a murmur spread round the boats and increased to what was more a shout of relief than a cheer.

The water was beginning to bubble, as if in a giant saucepan; it boiled and frothed and eddied, and then suddenly broke and disappeared and became fish. It was the miracle of Galilee enacted over again in the light of a Cornish moon. There was no water any more: only fish, as big as herrings, jumbled together in their thousands, jumping, wriggling, glinting, fighting and twisting to escape.

The net heaved and lurched, the big boats heeled over as the men strained to hold the catch. People talking and shouting, the splash of oars, the excited shouts of the fishers; the earlier noise was nothing to this.

The tuck net was now fast and the fishermen were already dipping baskets into the net and tipping them full of fish into the bottom of the boat. It seemed as if everyone was mindful of the haste necessary to take full advantage of good fortune. It was as if a storm waited just over the summit of the nearest cliff. Two big flat-bottomed boats like barges were ferried alongside and men hanging over the side began to work with fury to fill them. Other small boats quickly surrounded the net to take in the catch.

Sometimes the moonlight seemed to convert the fish into heaps of coins, and to Ross it looked like sixty or eighty darkfaced sub-human pygmies scooping at an inexhaustible bag of silver.

Soon men were up to their ankles in pilchards, soon up to their knees. Boats broke away and were rowed gingerly towards the shore, their gunnels no more than two inches above the lapping water. On shore the activity was no less; lanterns were everywhere while the fish were shovelled into wheelbarrows and hurried towards the salting cellars for picking over and inspection. Still the work round the net went on amongst the springing gleaming fish.

At the other side of the bay another but lesser catch was being hauled in. Ross and Demelza ate their cakes and took a sip of brandy from the same flask and talked in lowered voices of what they saw.

'Home now?' Ross said presently.

'A small bit longer,' Demelza suggested. 'The night is so warm. It is grand to be 'ere.'

He dipped his oars gently and straightened the bows of the boat towards the gentle lift and fall of the sea. They had drifted away from the crowds of boats, and it rather pleased him to get this detached view.

He found, quite to his surprise, that he was happy. Not merely happy in Demelza's happiness but in himself. He couldn't think why. The condition just existed within him.

. . . They waited and watched until the tuck net was almost cleared and the fishermen were going to lower it again. Then they waited to see if the second haul would be as big as the first. Whenever they were about to leave some fresh interest held them. Time passed unnoticed while the moon on its downward path came near the coast line and picked out a silver stitching on the water.

At last Ross slowly exerted his strength on the oars

and the boat began to move. As they passed near the others Pally Rogers recognized them and called, 'Good night!' Some of the others paused, sweating from their labours and also shouted.

'Good catch, eh, Pally?' Ross said.

''Andsome. More'n a quarter of a million fish, I reckon, afore we're done.'

'I'm very glad. It will make a difference next winter.'

'Night, sur.'

'Good night.'

'Night, sur.'

'Night . . .'

They rowed away, and as they went the sounds of all the voices and human activity slowly faded, into a smaller space, into a little confined murmur in the great night. They rowed out towards the open sea and the sharp cliffs and the black dripping rocks.

'Everyone is happy tonight,' Ross said, half to himself.

Demelza's face gleamed in the stern. 'They like you,' she said in an undertone. 'Everyone d' like you.'

He grunted. 'Little silly.'

'No, tis the truth. I know because I'm one of 'em. You and your father was different from the others. But mostly you. You're – you're—' She stumbled. 'You're half a gent and half one of them. And then you trying to help Jim Carter and giving food to people—'

'And marrying you.'

They passed into the shadow of the cliffs. 'No, not

that,' she said soberly. 'Maybe they don't like that. But they like you all the same.'

'You're too sleepy to talk sense,' he said. 'Cover your head and doze off till we're home.'

She did not obey, but sat watching the dark line where the shadow of the land ended and the glinting water began. She would have preferred to be out there. The shadow had lengthened greatly since they came out, and she would have rather made a wide circuit to keep within the friendly light of the moon. She stared into the deep darkness of one of the deserted coves they were passing. To these places no man ever came. They were desolate and cold. She could picture unholy things living there, spirits of the dead, things come out of the sea. She shivered and turned away.

Ross said: 'Take another nip of brandy.'

'No.' She shook her head. 'No. Not cold, Ross.'

In a few minutes they were turning into Nampara Cove. The boat slipped through the ripples at the edge and grounded in the sand. He got out and as she made to follow caught her about the waist and carried her to dry land. He kissed her before he put her down.

When the boat was drawn up into its cave and the oars hidden where a casual vagrant could not find them he rejoined her where she was waiting just above high-water mark. For a while neither of them made a move and they watched the moon set. As it neared the water it began to grow misshapen and discoloured like an overripe blood orange squeezed between sea and sky. The silver sword across the sea became tarnished and shrank until it was gone and only the old moon remained, bloated and dark, sinking into the mists.

Then without words they turned, walked across the sand and shingle, crossed the stream at the stepping-stones and walked together hand in hand the half mile to the house.

She was quite silent. He had never done what he had done tonight. He had never kissed her before except in passion. This was something different. She knew him to be closer to her tonight than he had ever been before. For the very first time they were on a level. It was not Ross Poldark, gentleman farmer, of Nampara, and his maid, whom he had married because it was better than being alone. They were a man and a woman, with no inequality between them. She was older than her years and he younger; and they walked home hand in hand through the slanting shadows of the new darkness.

I am happy, he thought again. Something is happening to me, to us, transmuting our shabby little love affair. Keep this mood, hold on to it. No slipping back.

The only sound all the way home was the bubbling of the stream beside their path. The house greeted them whitely. Moths fluttered away to the stars and the trees stood silent and black.

BRAM STOKER
(1847–1912)

We've got something of a trek before our next stop, so how about a bit of a wild and weird story? Now, except for the fact that his wife Florence was born in Falmouth, the *Dracula* author's connections to the region are slim, yet Cornwall features prominently in two of his tales: the novel *The Jewel of Seven Stars* and the short story 'The Coming of Abel Behenna'. The latter is a little coastal melodrama, but the former is Stoker at his most extravagantly bonkers. Here, Cornwall is a kind of wild hinterland, far removed from civilized London, so remote that one might get away with almost anything – even clandestine occult rituals for resurrecting Egyptian mummies.

We join the party as they travel from London to Abel Trelawney's Cornish estate for his Great Experiment. Trelawney brings the eponymous jewel and a mummified cat, while his daughter Margaret takes the astral body of the dead Queen Tera, who is currently possessing her. It is Bram Stoker, after all . . .

from The Jewel of Seven Stars

We arrived at Westerton about nine o'clock in the evening. Carts and horses were in waiting, and the work of unloading the train began at once. Our own party did not wait to see the work done, as it was in the hands of competent people. We took the carriage which was in waiting, and through the darkness of the night sped on to Kyllion.

We were all impressed by the house as it appeared in the bright moonlight. A great gray stone mansion of the Jacobean period; vast and spacious, standing high over the sea on the very verge of a high cliff. When we had swept round the curve of the avenue cut through the rock, and come out on the high plateau on which the house stood, the crash and murmur of waves breaking against rock far below us came with an invigorating breath of moist sea air. We understood then in an instant how well we were shut out from the world on that rocky shelf above the sea.

[...]

We had supper in the great dining-room on the south side, the walls of which actually hung over the sea. The murmur came up muffled, but it never ceased. As the little promontory stood well out into the sea, the northern side of the house was open; and the due north was in no way shut out by the great mass of rock, which reared high above us, shut out the rest of the world. Far off across the bay we could see the trembling lights of the castle, and here and there along the shore the faint light of a fisher's window. For the rest the sea was a dark blue plain with here and there a flicker of light as the gleam of starlight fell on the slope of a swelling wave.

When supper was over we all adjourned to the room which Mr. Trelawny had set aside as his study, his bedroom being close to it. As we entered, the first thing I noticed was a great safe, somewhat similar to that which stood in his room in London. When we were in the room Mr. Trelawny went over to the table, and, taking out his pocket-book, laid it on the table. As he did so he pressed down on it with the palm of his hand. A strange pallor came over his face. With fingers that trembled he opened the book, saying as he did so:

"Its bulk does not seem the same; I hope nothing has happened!"

All three of us men crowded round close. Margaret alone remained calm; she stood erect and silent, and still as a statue. She had a far-away look in her eyes, as though she did not either know or care what was going on around her.

With a despairing gesture Trelawny threw open the pouch of the pocket-book wherein he had placed the Jewel of Seven Stars. As he sank down on the chair which stood close to him, he said in a hoarse voice:

"My God! it is gone. Without it the Great Experiment can come to nothing!"

His words seemed to wake Margaret from her introspective mood. An agonised spasm swept her face; but almost on the instant she was calm. She almost smiled as she said:

"You may have left it in your room, Father. Perhaps it has fallen out of the pocket-book whilst you were changing." Without a word we all hurried into the next room through the open door between the study and the bedroom. And then a sudden calm fell on us like a cloud of fear.

There! on the table, lay the Jewel of Seven Stars, shining and sparkling with lurid light, as though each of the seven points of each of the seven stars gleamed through blood!

Timidly we each looked behind us, and then at each other. Margaret was now like the rest of us. She had lost her statuesque calm. All the introspective rigidity had gone from her; and she clasped her hands together till the knuckles were white.

Without a word Mr. Trelawny raised the Jewel, and hurried with it into the next room. As quietly as he could he opened the door of the safe with the key fastened to his wrist and placed the Jewel within. When the heavy doors were closed and locked he seemed to breathe more freely.

Somehow this episode, though a disturbing one in many ways, seemed to bring us back to our old selves. Since we had left London we had all been overstrained; and this was a sort of relief. Another step in our strange enterprise had been effected.

The change back was more marked in Margaret than in any of us. Perhaps it was that she was a woman, whilst we were men; perhaps it was that she was younger than the rest; perhaps both reasons were effective, each in its own way. At any rate the change was there, and I was happier than I had been through the long journey. All her buoyancy, her tenderness, her deep feeling seemed to shine forth once more; now and again as her Father's eyes rested on her, his face seemed to light up.

Whilst we waited for the carts to arrive, Mr. Trelawny took us through the house, pointing out and explaining where the objects which we had brought with us were to be placed. In one respect only did he withhold confidence. The positions of all those things which had connection with the Great Experiment were not indicated. The cases containing them were to be left in the outer hall, for the present.

By the time we had made the survey, the carts began to arrive; and the stir and bustle of the previous night were renewed. Mr. Trelawny stood in the hall beside the massive iron-bound door, and gave directions as to the placing of each of the great packing-cases. Those containing many items were placed in the inner hall where they were to be unpacked.

[...]

Mr. Trelawny, having seen the doors locked, took us into the study.

"Now," said he when we were seated, "I have a secret to impart; but, according to an old promise which does not leave me free, I must ask you each to give me a solemn promise not to reveal it. For three hundred years at least such a promise has been exacted from every one to whom it was told, and more than once life and safety were secured through loyal observance of the promise. Even as it is, I am breaking the spirit, if not the letter of the tradition; for I should only tell it to the immediate members of my family."

We all gave the promise required. Then he went on:

"There is a secret place here, a cave, natural originally but finished by labor, underneath the house. I will not undertake to say that it has always been used according to the law. During the Bloody Assize more than a few Cornishmen found refuge in it; and later, and earlier, it formed, I have no doubt whatever, a useful place for storing contraband goods. 'Tre Pol and Pen,' I suppose you know, have always been smugglers; and their relations and friends and neighbors have not held back from the enterprise. For all such reasons a safe hiding-place was always considered a valuable possession; and as the heads of our House have always insisted on preserving the secret, I am in honor bound to it. Later on, if all be well, I shall of course tell you, Margaret, and you too, Ross, under the conditions that I am bound to make."

He rose up, and we all followed him. Leaving us in the outer hall, he went away alone for a few minutes; and returning, beckoned us to follow him.

In the inside hall we found a whole section of an outstanding angle moved away, and from the cavity saw a great hole dimly dark, and the beginning of a rough staircase cut in the rock. As it was not pitch dark there was manifestly some means of lighting it naturally, so without pause we followed our host as he descended. After some forty or fifty steps cut in a winding passage, we came to a great cave whose further end tapered away into blackness. It was a huge place, dimly lit by a few irregular long slits of eccentric shape. Manifestly these were faults in the rock which would easily allow the windows to be disguised from without. Close to each of them was a hanging shutter which could be swung across by means of a dangling rope. The sound of the ceaseless beat of the waves came up muffled from far below. Mr. Trelawny at once began to speak:

"This is the spot which I have chosen, as the best I know, for the scene of our Great Experiment. In a hundred different ways it fulfils the conditions which I am led to believe are primary with regard to success. Here, we are, and shall be, as isolated as Queen Tera herself would have been in her rocky tomb in the Valley of the Sorcerer, and still in a rocky cavern. For good or ill we must here stand by our chances, and abide by results. If we are successful we shall be able to let in on the world of modern science such a flood of light from the Old World as will change every condition of thought and experiment and practice. If we fail, then even the knowledge of our attempt will die with us. For this, and all else which may come, I believe we are prepared!" He paused. No one spoke, but we all bowed our heads gravely in acquiescence. He resumed, but with a certain hesitancy:

"It is not yet too late! If any of you have a doubt or a misgiving, for God's sake, speak it now! Whoever it may be, can go hence without let or hindrance. The rest of us can go on our way alone!"

Again he paused, and looked keenly at us in turn. We looked at each other; but no one quailed. For my own part, if I had had any doubt as to going on, the look on Margaret's face would have reassured me. It was fearless; it was intense; it was full of a divine calm.

Mr. Trelawny took a long breath, and in a more cheerful, as well as in a more decided tone, went on:

"As we are all of one mind, the sooner we get the necessary matters in train the better. Let me tell you that this place, like all the rest of the house, can be lit with electricity. We could not join the wires to the mains lest our secret should become known, but I have a cable here which we can attach in the hall and complete the circuit!" As he was speaking, be began to ascend the steps. From close to the entrance he took the end of a cable; this he drew forward and attached to a switch in the wall. Then, turning on a tap, he flooded the whole vault and staircase below with light.

[...]

We set to work at once; and before nightfall had lowered, had unbooked, and placed in the positions designated for each by Trelawny, all the great sarcophagi and all the curios and other matters which we had taken with us.

It was a strange and weird proceeding the placing of those wonderful monuments of a by-gone age in that great cavern, which represented in its cutting and purpose and up-to-date mechanism and electric lights both the old world and the new. But as time went on I grew more and more to recognise the wisdom and correctness of Mr. Trelawny's choice. I was much disturbed when Silvio, who had been brought into the cave in the arms of his mistress, and who was lying asleep on my coat which I had taken off, sprang up when the cat mummy had been unpacked, and flew at it with the same ferocity which he had previously exhibited. The incident showed Margaret in a new phase, and one which gave my heart a pang. She bad been standing quite still at one side of the cave leaning on a sarcophagus, in one of those fits of abstraction which had of late come upon her; but on hearing the sound, and seeing Silvio's violent onslaught, she seemed to fall into a positive fury of passion. Her eyes blazed, and her mouth took a hard, cruel tension which was new to me. Instinctively she stepped towards Silvio as if to interfere in the attack. But I too had stepped forward; and as she caught my eye a strange spasm came upon her, and she stopped. Its intensity made me hold my breath; and I put up my hand to clear my eyes. When I had done this, she had on the instant recovered her calm, and there was a look of brief wonder on her face. With all her old grace and sweetness she swept over and lifted Silvio, just as she had done on former occasions, and held him in her arms, petting him and treating him as though he were a little child who had erred.

As I looked a strange fear came over me. The Margaret that I knew seemed to be changing; and in my inmost heart I prayed that the disturbing cause might soon come to an end. More than ever I longed at that moment that our terrible Experiment should come to a prosperous termination.

When all had been arranged in the room as Mr. Trelawny wished he turned to us, one after another, till he had concentrated the intelligence of us all upon him. Then he said:

"All is now ready in this place. We must only await the proper time to begin."

[...]

And so we waited only for the 31st of July, the next day but one, when the Great Experiment would be made.

THE MAY DAY SONGS OF PADSTOW
collected by Robert Hunt

It feels like we were only just celebrating May in Helston, but here we are in Padstow for May Day, with singing and dancing and the processions of the red and the blue 'Osses that prance about the streets capturing young women while being followed by the people of Padstow, who are dressed all in white except for red or blue neckerchiefs, depending which 'Oss the family follows.

Singing begins at midnight on May Eve with 'The Night Song', which Robert Hunt, in the version presented here from his *Popular Romances of the West of England*, calls 'The Morning Song'.

The Morning Song

Unite and unite and let us all unite,
    For summer it is come unto day;
And whither we are going we all will unite
    In the merry morning of May.

Arise up, Mr. —, and joy you betide,
    For summer is come unto day;
And bright is your bride that lays by your side
    In the merry morning of May.

Arise up, Mrs. —, and gold be your ring,
    For summer is come unto day;
And give to us a cup of ale, the merrier we shall sing
    In the merry morning of May.

Arise up, Miss —, all in your smock of silk,
    For summer is come unto day;
And all your body under as white as any milk,
    In the merry morning of May.

The young men of Padstow might, if they would,
    For summer is come unto day;
They might have built a ship and gilded her with gold
    In the merry morning of May.

Now fare you well, and we bid you good cheer,
    For summer is come unto day;
We will come no more unto your house before another
      year,
    In the merry morning of May.

The Day Song

Awake, St. George, our English knight,
  For summer is a-come O, and winter is a go;
And every day God give us His grace
  By day and by night O!

Where is St. George, where is he O?
  He is out in his long boat all on the salt sea O!
And in every land O! the land where'er we go,
  And for to fetch the summer home.
            The summer and the May O,
            For summer is a come,
            And winter is a go.

Where are the French dogs that make such boast O?
  They shall eat the grey goose feather,
And we will cattle roast O!
  And in every land O! the land where'er we go,
            The summer and the May O.

Thou mightst have shown thy knavish face!
  Thou mightst have tarried at home O!
But thou shalt be an old cuckold,
  And thou shalt wear the horns O;
            The summer and the May O.

With hal-an-tow and jolly rumble O,

For summer is a come O, and winter is a go,
And in every land O, the land where'er we go,
Up flies the kite, and down falls the lark O!

Aunt Ursula Birdhood she had an old ewe,
And she died in her own park O!

And for to fetch the summer home.

Thomas Hardy
(1840–1928)

Hardy came to St Juliot to fix the church but he ended
up marrying the rector's sister-in-law. As a result, Cornwall features with fair prominence in his writing – both
the poetry and the prose – especially this lovely stretch
of the north coast.

The following few poems are from a sequence written much later in life, recalling those early days when
he and Emma wandered the cliffs of Boscastle and
Beeny. But rather than being celebratory, the poems are
filled with sadness, written immediately after Emma's
death, when Hardy was feeling great regret for his treat-
ment of her.

I Found Her Out There

I found her out there
On a slope few see,
That falls westwardly
To the salt-edged air,
Where the ocean breaks
On the purple strand,
And the hurricane shakes
The solid land.

I brought her here,
And have laid her to rest
In a noiseless nest
No sea beats near.
She will never be stirred
In her loamy cell
By the waves long heard
And loved so well.

So she does not sleep
By those haunted heights
The Atlantic smites
And the blind gales sweep,
Whence she often would gaze
At Dundagel's famed head,

While the dipping blaze
Dyed her face fire-red;

And would sigh at the tale
Of sunk Lyonnesse,
As a wind-tugged trees
Flapped her cheek like a flail;
Or listen at whiles
With a thought-bound brow
To the murmuring miles
She is far from now.

Yet her shade, maybe,
Will creep underground
Till it catch the sound
Of that western sea
As it swells and sobs
Where she once domiciled,
And joy in its throbs
With the heart of a child.

Beeny Cliff

MARCH 1870–MARCH 1913

I

O the opal and the sapphire of that wandering western
    sea,
And the woman riding high above with bright hair
    flapping free—
The woman whom I loved so, and who loyally
    loved me.

II

The pale mews plained below us, and the waves
    seemed far away
In a nether sky, engrossed in saying their ceaseless
    babbling say,
As we laughed light-heartedly aloft on that clear-
    sunned March day.

III

A little cloud then cloaked us, and there flew an
    irised rain,
And the Atlantic dyed its levels with a dull
    misfeatured stain,

And then the sun burst out again, and purples prinked
    the main.

IV

—Still in all its chasmal beauty bulks old Beeny to
    the sky,
And shall she and I not go there once again now
    March is nigh,
And the sweet things said in that March say anew
    there by and by?

V

What if still in chasmal beauty looms that wild weird
    western shore,
The woman now is—elsewhere—whom the ambling
    pony bore,
And nor knows nor cares for Beeny, and will laugh
    there nevermore.

At Castle Boterel

As I drive to the junction of lane and highway,
　And the drizzle bedrenches the waggonette,
I look behind at the fading byway,
　And see on its slope, now glistening wet,
　　　Distinctly yet

Myself and a girlish form benighted
　In dry March weather. We climb the road
Beside a chaise. We had just alighted
　To ease the sturdy pony's load
　　　When he sighed and slowed.

What we did as we climbed, and what we talked of
　Matters not much, nor to what it led,—
Something that life will not be balked of
　Without rude reason till hope is dead,
　　　And feeling fled.

It filled but a minute. But was there ever
　A time of such quality, since or before,
In that hill's story? To one mind never,
　Though it has been climbed, foot-swift, foot-sore,
　　　By thousands more.

Primaeval rocks form the road's steep border,
　And much have they faced there, first and last,

Of the transitory in Earth's long order;
　　But what they record in colour and cast
　　　　Is—that we two passed.

And to me, though Time's unflinching rigour,
　　In mindless rote, has ruled from sight
The substance now, one phantom figure
　　Remains on the slope, as when that night
　　　　Saw us alight.

I look and see it there, shrinking, shrinking,
　　I look back at it amid the rain
For the very last time; for my sand is sinking,
　　And I shall traverse old love's domain
　　　　Never again.

CHARLES CAUSLEY
(1917–2003)

We've got to nip inland to meet Mr Causley, our best beloved poet. He spent his adult life as a schoolteacher in Launceston, save for those navy years in the Second World War that so influenced his poetry.

Angel Hill is a real place. If you walk up from Causley's cottage on Ridgegrove Hill and cross the road at that horrible blind corner you'll find yourself on Angel Hill. It's said it got its name when a visiting bishop who was passing slowly up the incline in his coach was woken by St Mary's Minstrels, who had gathered at the top to welcome him. Being roused abruptly, and perhaps a little disoriented, the bishop proclaimed the voices to be a choir of angels.

It's a poem typical of Causley. On the surface it is easy to read, attractive and buoyant with a natural rhythm, but underneath all that there is something else – something more unsettling – going on . . .

Angel Hill

A sailor came walking down Angel Hill,
He knocked on my door with a right good will,
With a right good will he knocked on my door.
He said, 'My friend, we have met before.'
    No, never, said I.

He searched my eye with a sea-blue stare
And he laughed aloud on the Cornish air,
On the Cornish air he laughed aloud
And he said, 'My friend, you have grown too proud.'
    No, never, said I.

'In war we swallowed the bitter bread
And drank of the brine,' the sailor said.
'We took of the bread and we tasted the brine
As I bound your wounds and you bound mine.'
    No, never, said I.

'By day and night on the diving sea
We whistled to sun and moon,' said he.
'Together we whistled to moon and sun
And vowed our stars should be as one.'
    No, never, said I.

'And now,' he said, 'that the war is past
I come to your hearth and home at last.
I come to your home and hearth to share
Whatever fortune waits me there.'

    No, never, said I.

'I have no wife nor son,' he said,
'Nor pillow on which to lay my head,
No pillow have I, nor wife nor son,
Till you shall give to me my own.'

    No, never, said I.

His eye it flashed like a lightning-dart
And still as a stone then stood my heart.
My heart as a granite stone was still
And he said, 'My friend, but I think you will.'

    No, never, said I.

The sailor smiled and turned in his track
And shifted the bundle on his back
And I heard him sing as he strolled away,
'You'll send and you'll fetch me one fine day.'

    No, never, said I.

R. S. HAWKER
(1803–1875)

This is it folks, our final stop. I hope you've enjoyed the journey. It's been some spectacular scenery, hasn't it? Pay close attention now. We might be near the border but here is one of our more imposing figures, a dramatic poet and preacher, the Reverend Hawker.

Hawker was the vicar of the remote clifftop church of St Morwenna and St John the Baptist here at Morwenstow, from 1835 until his death, and living along this stretch of coast meant Hawker saw his share of death, with corpses and body parts from wrecked ships washing up on the beach, which he would collect and bring back to the church for proper burial.

His poetry is mostly set in Cornwall and reflects the life he led – confirmation and baptism in the parish, the stories of saints and legends, religious themes – an attractive mix of the epic and the everyday, with death never far away. Let's begin with Hawker's epic Arthurian quest and end with a shout of Trelawny.

from The Quest of the Sangraal

So forth they fare, King Arthur and his men,
Like stout quaternions of the Maccabee:
They halt, and form at craggy Carradon;
Fit scene for haughty hope and stern farewell.
Lo! the rude altar, and the rough-hewn rock,
The grim and ghastly semblance of the fiend,
His haunt and coil within that pillar'd home.
Hark! the wild echo! Did the demon breathe
That yell of vengeance from the conscious stone?

There the brown barrow curves its sullen breast,
Above the bones of some dead Gentile's soul:
All husht—and calm—and cold—until anon
Gleams the old dawn—the well-remembered day—
Then may you hear, beneath that hollow cairn,
The clash of arms: the muffled shout of war;
Blent with the rustle of the kindling dead!

They stand—and hush their hearts to hear the King.
Then said he, like a prince of Tamar-land—
Around his soul, Dundagel and the sea—

"Ha! Sirs—ye seek a noble crest to-day,
To win and wear the starry Sangraal,
The link that binds to God a lonely land.

Would that my arm went with you, like my heart!
But the true shepherd must not shun the fold:
For in this flock are crouching grievous wolves,
And chief among them all, my own false kin.
Therefore I tarry by the cruel sea,
To hear at eve the treacherous mermaid's song,
And watch the wallowing monsters of the wave,—
'Mid all things fierce, and wild, and strange, alone!

"Ay! all beside can win companionship:
The churl may clip his mate beneath the thatch,
While his brown urchins nestle at his knees:
The soldier give and grasp a mutual palm,
Knit to his flesh in sinewy bonds of war:
The knight may seek at eve his castle-gate,
Mount the old stair, and lift the accustom'd latch,
To find, for throbbing brow and weary limb,
That paradise of pillows, one true breast:
But he, the lofty ruler of the land,
Like yonder Tor, first greeted by the dawn,
And wooed the latest by the lingering day,
With happy homes and hearths beneath his breast,
Must soar and gleam in solitary snow.
The lonely one is, evermore, the King.
So now farewell, my lieges, fare ye well,
And God's sweet Mother be your benison!
Since by grey Merlin's gloss, this wondrous cup
Is, like the golden vase in Aaron's ark,
A fount of manha for a yearning world,
As full as it can hold of God and heaven,

Search the four winds until the balsam breathe,
Then grasp, and fold it in your very soul!

"I have no son, no daughter of my loins,
To breathe, 'mid future men, their father's name:
My blood will perish when these veins are dry;
Yet am I fain some deeds of mine should live—
I would not be forgotten in this land:
I yearn that men I know not, men unborn,
Should find, amid these fields, King Arthur's fame!
Here let them say, by proud Dundagel's walls—
'They brought the Sangraal back by his command,
They touched these rugged rocks with hues of
    God:'
So shall my name have worship, and my land.

"Ah! native Cornwall! throned upon the hills,
Thy moorland pathways worn by Angel feet,
Thy streams that march in music to the sea
'Mid Ocean's merry noise, his billowy laugh!
Ah me! a gloom falls heavy on my soul—
The birds that sung to me in youth are dead;
I think, in dreamy vigils of the night,
It may be God is angry with my land,
Too much athirst for fame, too fond of blood;
And all for earth, for shadows, and the dream
To glean an echo from the winds of song!

"But now, let hearts be high! the Archangel held
A tournay with the fiend on Abarim,

And good Saint Michael won his dragon-crest!

"Be this our cry! the battle is for God!
If bevies of foul fiends withstand your path,
Nay! if strong angels hold the watch and ward,
Plunge in their midst, and shout, 'A Sangraal!'"

Death Song

There lies a cold corpse upon the sands
  Down by the rolling sea;
Close up the eyes and straighten the hands,
  As a Christian man's should be.

Bury it deep, for the good of my soul,
  Six feet below the ground;
Let the sexton come and the death-bell toll,
  And good men stand around.

Lay it among the churchyard stones,
  Where the priest hath blessed the clay;
I cannot leave the unburied bones,
  And I fain would go my way.

The Wail of the Cornish Mother

"In Ramah there was a voice heard."

They say 'tis a sin to sorrow—
  That what God doth is best:
But 'tis only a month to-morrow,
  I buried it from my breast.

I know it should be a pleasure,
  Your child to God to send;
But mine was a precious treasure
  To me and to my poor friend.

I thought it would call me "mother,"
  The very first words it said;
Oh! I never can love another
  Like the blessèd babe that's dead.

Well, God is its own dear Father,
  It was carried to church and blessed:
And our Saviour's arms will gather
  Such children to their rest.

I shall make my best endeavour
  That my sins may be forgiven;
I will serve God more than ever,
  To meet my child in heaven.

I will check this foolish sorrow,
   For what God does is best;
But Oh! 'tis a month to-morrow,
   I buried it from my breast.

The Song of the Western Men

I

A good sword and a trusty hand!
  A merry heart and true!
King James's men shall understand
  What Cornish lads can do!

II

And have they fix'd the where and when?
  And shall Trelawny die?
Here's twenty thousand Cornish men
  Will see the reason why!

III

Out spake their Captain brave and bold,
  A merry wight was he:
"If London Tower were Michael's hold,
  We'll set Trelawny free!"

IV

"We'll cross the Tamar, land to land,
  The Severn is no stay—

All side by side, and hand to hand,
  And who shall bid us nay?

V

"And when we come to London Wall,
  A pleasant sight to view,
Come forth! Come forth, ye Cowards all,
  To better men than you!

VI

"Trelawny he's in keep and hold,
  Trelawny he may die;
But here's twenty thousand Cornish bold,
  Will see the reason why!"

Permissions Acknowledgements

MACMILLAN COLLECTOR'S LIBRARY

**Own the world's great works of literature in
one beautiful collectible library**

Designed and curated to appeal to book lovers everywhere,
Macmillan Collector's Library editions are small enough to
travel with you and striking enough to take pride of place
on your bookshelf. These much-loved literary classics
also make the perfect gift.

Beautifully produced with gilt edges, a ribbon marker,
bespoke illustrated cover and real cloth binding, every
Macmillan Collector's Library hardback adheres to the
same high production values.

Discover something new or cherish your favourite
stories with this elegant collection.

**Macmillan Collector's Library:
own, collect, and treasure**

Discover the full range at
macmillancollectorslibrary.com